REVIEWS OF MARTHA MOODY

"One of Stinson's triumphs is to make Amanda's fairy-tale success as a writer seem completely plausible amid the vivid depiction of the grime and hard work of her life as first a farmer's wife, then a single woman struggling to survive on the small homestead." — Margot Livesey, *Scotland on Sunday*

"A tale of longing and self identification and reconciliation. Amanda Linger pines for shop owner Martha Moody whose girth, sensuous folds of flesh and loving caresses pull Amanda out of the stasis of a loveless marriage . . . *Martha Moody* is a tender exquisitely rendered story with strong characters, a sense of love and magic surrounding them, and one incredible cow." — *Icon Magazine*, Toronto

"Susan Stinson's deceptively svelte-seeming story is a lush comic masterpiece: a totally convincing celebration of the combined erotic power of untrammelled female flesh, forbidden sex and unleashed words." — *Mail on Sunday*, London

"*Martha Moody*, is a rich and complicated novel, nearly edible in its sensuous physicality." — *Sojourner*

"Stinson's follow-up to the utterly fantastic *Fat Girl Dances with Rocks* is so bloody good it made me want to run naked through a meadow." — *Time Out, London*

"Here we have a story of love spurned, uncommonly well told, in language that is rich and strange, erotic and fanciful. Set against the backdrop of Western frontier life, it's a powerful

tale of seeming betrayal, and the value of friendships between women. The best book yet from The Women's Press."
— *Gay Times,* London

"Stinson's celebration of the love and friendship of women deserves a larger audience than one made up of only lesbian feminists." — *Booklist*

"Remarkable story . . . Amanda's fictional Martha is a wild and magical creature who churns clouds into butter with her magnificent thighs and flies on the back of a fabulous winged cow." — *Bay Area Reporter*

"Susan Stinson writes as though she means every word to be tasted, savoured." — *Women's Library Newsletter*

"A jewel . . . Martha Moody is magnificent. She is unashamedly fat and she is beautiful, dignified and desirable. She will take her place in modern literature as a truly marvellous role model for large women. Never before have I encountered the large body depicted with such beauty."
— Shelley Bovey, *Yes Magazine,* UK

Martha Moody

ALSO BY SUSAN STINSON

Belly Songs
Fat Girl Dances with Rocks
Venus of Chalk
Spider in a Tree
Lamentation Hill (forthcoming)

Martha Moody

a novel

Susan Stinson

Small Beer Press
Easthampton, MA

This is a work of fiction. All characters and events portrayed
in this book are either fictitious or used fictitiously.

Martha Moody copyright © 1995 by Susan Stinson (susanstinson.net). All rights reserved. First published
by Spinsters Ink. First Small Beer Press edition published in 2020.

The following selected passages have been reprinted with permission of the author.
"Martha Moody," pp. 4-6, was previously published in *Word of Mouth: Short Short Stories* by Women, ed.
Irene Zahava (Freedom, Ca.: Crossing Press, 1990).
"Milk," pp. 35-37, first appeared in slightly different form in *Quickies: Lesbian Short-Shorts,* ed. Irene Za-
hava (Ithaca, N.Y.: Violet Ink, 1992). It also appeared in *The Body of Love,* ed. Tee A. Corinne (Austin,
Tex.: Banned Books, 1993).
"Cream," pp. 44-48, appeared in *Sinister Wisdom* 51 (Winter 1993-94).
"Young Martha in the River," pp. 84-85, was previously published in *Quickies: Lesbian Short-Shorts,* ed.
Irene Zahava (Ithaca, N.Y.: Violet Ink, 1992).
"Tell," pp. 112-114, appeared in a different form in *Sinister Wisdom* 50 (Summer/Fall 1993) and in
Susan Stinson, *Belly Songs: In Celebration of Fat Women* (Northampton, Mass.: Orogeny Press, 1993).

Small Beer Press
150 Pleasant Street #306
Easthampton, MA 01027
bookmoonbooks.com
weightlessbooks.com
smallbeerpress.com
info@smallbeerpress.com

Distributed to the trade by Consortium.

Library of Congress Cataloging-in-Publication Data

Names: Stinson, Susan, 1960- author.
Title: Martha Moody : a novel / Susan Stinson.
Description: First Small Beer Press edition. | Easthampton, MA : Small Beer
    Press, 2020. | Summary: "At once a love story and a lush comic
    masterpiece, Martha Moody is a speculative western which embraces the
    ordinary and gritty details - as well as the magic - of women's lives in
    the old west"-- Provided by publisher.
Identifiers: LCCN 2020033949 (print) | LCCN 2020033950 (ebook) | ISBN
    9781618731807 (paperback) | ISBN 9781618731814 (ebook)
Subjects: LCGFT: Novels.
Classification: LCC PS3569.T535 M37 2020 (print) | LCC PS3569.T535
    (ebook) | DDC 813/.54--dc23
LC record available at https://lccn.loc.gov/2020033949
LC ebook record available at https://lccn.loc.gov/2020033950

First edition 1 2 3 4 5 6 7 8 9

Text set in Centaur.
Printed on 50# Natures Natural 30% PCR Recycled Paper in the USA.
Cover illustration copyright © 2020 by Theo Black (theblackarts.com). All rights reserved.

For Elaine with love

One

I was crouched next to the creek baiting my hook with a hunk of fat when I heard a rustling on the bank upstream. I turned my head and saw Martha Moody looking into the water.

She was a heavy woman bound up with dry and perishable goods, the owner of Moody's General Store. Her red hair was pulled into a bun and she wore a black dress with jet buttons that reflected light.

I was embarrassed to be caught fishing on Sunday with mud on my skirt, so I hid behind a cottonwood. Martha leaned over, unlaced her shoes, and rolled down her stockings. I watched as she tucked them beneath the root of a tree, then bunched her skirt up in one hand and stepped into the water.

Dirt trickled into my collar from the bank, but I stood still. I could see the white blurs of her feet as she waded towards me. She moved with calm propriety: a large, plain, respectable woman from the nape of her neck down to her knees. She dropped her skirt. It floated and plastered itself to her shins, a changed, molded thing.

Martha moved more slowly as her skirt got soaked, but she was not ponderous, the way she was behind the counter at the store. When Martha said, "Don't lean on the glass," even the sheriff jumped back. Now she kicked at her hem, splashing herself a little and nearly slipping on a rock.

She stopped within breathing distance of me, at a spot where the water took a drop over rocks. Fish hid in the deep place behind the falling water, and I had been luring them onto my hook. Martha tucked a strand of hair behind her ear, squatted down and went over face first. I put my mouth against the tree bark to keep from calling out as she passed me, covered with white foam and scraping sand. She came up spitting and laughing, and grabbed the bank to hold herself under the falls.

I heard her say, "Frowsy," then laugh more. She sat in the stream bed with the water rushing down, rushing over her. The sky was blue against the hard edge of the bank. I opened my creel, seized a fish, and threw it back into the water. It skidded past her. She turned her face and another one slapped her neck, then washed on past. She got on her knees, sinking in the soft bottom, and fish after fish swam past her. Big silver, small brown.

Martha stood. I stepped into an open spot on the bank so she could see me reaching into the creel and tossing another fish into the water with a high arc. I straightened the bow at the waist of my old calico, then tilted the creel towards Martha to show her that it was empty except for a few wet rushes on the bottom.

She stared at me, dripping water, as silver flashed over her feet. "Mrs. Linger, why are you throwing fish?" Her tone was cool. I felt like a kid caught with a pocketful of lemon drops I hadn't paid for.

I walked down the bank to her, wiping my hands on my skirt. I couldn't think of a good lie. The truth was, I wanted to add those shining bits of life to the picture Martha Moody was making with the water. I knew when a moment was ripe, which was how I came to be fishing when most decent women were getting supper on the table. "Why are you in the creek?"

Martha touched her glistening buttons. "For the poetry of the moment."

I nodded and reached to help her onto the bank. She grabbed my fingers so hard that I thought she was going to pull me into the water with her, but she just held on and dug her feet deeper into the mud. "I'm not ready to get out, Amanda Linger. Are you coming in?"

I pulled my hand away and stuck it in my dry pocket. I never rose to a dare. Martha stood there like she was a tree that had been bending the water around her since before Jesus walked in his own thunder and waves. I could see the outline of her corset through the fabric of her dress. I picked up my fishing pole. "I have to get to my milking."

Martha pulled one foot loose from the mud and held it under the fall to rinse it. I could smell the wet fabric of her skirt. Her hair was still knotted away from her face. "Milk. Yes." Her chin was soft and white. "Good day, then, Mrs. Linger."

I climbed the bank, inspired. "Good day."

After I left Martha Moody standing in the water, I hurried to the barn without going to the house. Miss Alice was waiting for me at the fence, bawling and looking at me with her yellow-flecked eyes. Her days had a strict rhythm, and she hated it when I was late.

I walked towards her with a cow swagger, swishing my pole behind me like a tail, bawling in answer. I opened the gate and she lowered her head to butt against my hip. "All right, Alice, yes, Pretty Alice, I know you're hungry."

I brought her a bucket of oats, then stood next to her with my hands in my armpits to warm them before I pulled up the stool. I rubbed my face against her hide. She smelled live and pungent.

Miss Alice gave more milk if I had a story to tell. We had been through most of the Bible, with special attention to mentions of kine and golden calves, as I squatted next to her mornings and evenings working her teats. I talked to help Miss Alice let her milk down. If she held back, it soured her bag for the next milking.

That night I told her the history of Martha Moody as I understood it from the conjectures of the ladies of the town.

Before she founded Moody, Martha had been a woman who liked a good apple pie with thick cream, but didn't have the grass to feed a cow. She had dried milk, but never cream, and she had suffered from grasshoppers and sparseness of joy.

Martha herself had never been sparse. She had been a fat city girl with red hair, acquainted with the Bible but also with the pleasures of ices and store-bought tarts. She had eaten turtle soup. She had dressed in white to shoot a bow and arrow, and had hit the mark. Her prowess in the fashionable sport of archery pleased her father, who was a lapsed Methodist with a gold watch fob and social ambitions. But Martha had met Wilbur Moody in a dry goods store, and he had come around the counter to hand her a bolt of cornflower blue cloth. She was married to him in a dress of that material in the spring. She didn't miss the grey city she left with Wilbur, toting dry goods, but she did miss cream. She liked the West. She nodded at the big sky. She asked nothing of the mountains, except that they keep her pointed straight away from the city and let her survive the pass. She came a good distance, then said it was enough. She was walking beside the wagon, singing to herself in a dry voice that had carried her across a lot of country. Wilbur was up on the seat, driving the oxen. They reached a creek. Water was news and a reason to stop. There were some small trees, maybe from a seed dropped by some other traveller. Martha looked at the sharp limbs and grey bark, and decided that this was enough to satisfy her need for company. She would winter here. Wilbur was gold-hungry and land-bored. He'd seen enough water in the East, although he filled every container he could find with the stuff. The rest of the party put their wagons in a circle, built fires, and spoke against leaving Martha for dead. But she had provisions, time to dig a sod house before the ground froze, and she had gone as far as she was willing to go. Wilbur knew better than to speak of love, but he did mention family honor. The sound of the water bordered the night.

She took some bolts of material, and the panes of glass she had packed with good quilts for padding, because she thought windows were worth the trouble and cold they leaked. She took a barrel of beans and a barrel of meal, and the dried milk. Wilbur poured half of each packet of seed into its own tin cup and lined them up in front of her on the ground.

"Martha," he said, "you can't live on seeds and water, so I hope you can live on your fat."

"I'll need Shakespeare and the Bible," she said. He gave her a hand digging a hole for a shelter, shoring it up with posts that came off the siding of the wagon. The rest of the party was already a morning ahead, so he looked into her brown eyes, wishing they were cornflower blue, gave her a kiss and rode off, rattling.

Martha picked up her shovel, thinking of barrel tables and barrel chairs, without a thought of who she might be cheating in claiming this land or who she might be seeding in her dry goods store by the stream. She didn't bother with naming, either, but people passing, and those staying, said "Moody" to tell where they were.

Miss Alice turned and stretched her neck until she was breathing on my shoulder. Her breath smelled fermented, like oat wine. I scratched her cheek and said, "I have a carnal attraction." Miss Alice put her soft nose against my dress. I rubbed her face a moment more, then stood up. "You're a fine cow, Miss Alice." I hung the stool on its peg and picked up the bucket. Miss Alice was watching me with her interested eyes, so I gave her a song about darling Clementine.

The sound of a horn came in behind my voice. I swung around to see my husband John in the barn door. I stopped singing, and he took the tune on.

John was a thin man, but he pushed full-bellied notes out of that horn. His cheeks held themselves tight to his bones and his cowlick caught light. I set the bucket on the shelf for the cream to rise, with a board across it to keep the flies out. Miss Alice sashayed out of her stall, rustling hay, and we both listened as John played dips and circles in the air with the chorus.

I sang the last bit about being dreadful sorry.

John lowered his horn and smiled at Miss Alice. "You like music, don't you, Alice? Sweetens the milk." He put his high pink forehead down to hers, and I had to laugh and take the ease of the moment for what it was—the soft rind of a cold marriage. We tended to Miss Alice with clear faces and knowing hearts. I did all the milking, but we both loved her.

John took the stiff brush from its hook and ran it along her yellow flank. I watched with something close to tenderness, then tugged on one of Miss Alice's ears. "I'd best see to supper. The band's coming to practice?"

He nodded without looking up. "I've already eaten. We'll be at it late."

I lit a lantern and hung it in the doorway, then left him still combing her side. As I walked up the hill to the house, I saw the other members of the Oddfellows Temperance Brass Band cutting across the fields in the dusk to join him. I stood on my high ground and gave them a wave, then hurried past the garden to the dark house.

I had cold meat and biscuits for supper, but I made a fire in the stove after I ate. In my working youth I had drunk a glass of wine after dinner with Mrs. Luz at the boarding house, but now I took nothing stronger than red clover tea. Sour music floated over the garden to me as I sipped; the band was working up new hymns. It was a chill night, and I thought of how cold the water must have been on Martha's feet. She hadn't flinched, though—she had laughed. Once the coal's blue flame burned down, I closed the dampers and sat next to the stove with my sewing chest. I was ripping apart my maroon merino to make over trimmed with black cord, but the music unsettled me, so after a time I put my sewing aside and took up paper and pen to copy passages from the Bible.

It pleased me to know the book chapter and verse. I loved it when God brought streams out of the rocks and caused waters to run down like rivers in the desert. I had dreamed more than once of the woman holding a cup as she rode a seven-headed beast. I got shivers from "In the beginning was the Word, and the Word was with God, and the Word was God." Forming the shapes of the words myself gave me comfort, like holding a rock smoothed in a stream.

I copied from the book of John the Apostle: the story of Lazarus raised from the dead. I loved it when the gathered mourners went to the grave. Jesus said, "Take ye away the stone." Martha, the practical sister of Lazarus, said, "Lord, by this time he stinketh."

That struck me as the words of a woman who had dealt with bad meat. I thought of white quivers of maggots in the saltpork. The Bible names pulled at me with their echoes of live names of people I knew: John, Martha, even Lazarus sounded a little like Miss Alice.

Jesus came to supper with alive-again Lazarus sitting at the table all unwrapped and washed up. Martha served the meal. My eyes ran back over the part about what the other sister, Mary, did, then I smoothed the paper in my lap and read it in my own hand:

> *Then took Mary a pound of ointment of spikenard, very costly, and anointed the feet of Jesus, and wiped his feet with her hair: and the house was filled with the odour of the ointment.*

It gave me a shiver. I pictured it: a grown woman approaching a man she knew to be holy, kneeling at the table in front of her sister and brother and their guests, and rubbing the Lord's bare feet. Did they take off their shoes before they sat down at the table? She must have at least felt the resentment of her sister as she warmed the oil in her hands and spread it over his soles, moving the skin in small circles to work out the cramps from the road. She kept her eyes on his feet, tracing the ridges between bones, taking her time.

The fire was low in the stove, but I didn't get up to tend it. I marked the place in the Bible with a bit of black cord, and closed my eyes. I saw it at first from a distance, as if I were Martha in the doorway of the kitchen: Jesus calm, receiving a tribute; the faces around the table, some tense, some indulgent; the muscles working in my sister's back as she bends and presses with her reckless patience. I leave Martha to move closer. In my dream, Mary rinses mud from his foot with clear water. The rich smell of the oil rises. I follow the weave in the fabric of Mary's robe over her shoulders down her arms to her brown fingers rolling his toes, relaxing the joints. She holds one foot between her palms, still for a long moment.

I was almost asleep. The coals were quiet. Mary pulls the leather tie from her hair and lets it fall over the Lord's foot. She closes the strands in her fist to gather it into a thickness, then uses her hair to wipe the oil from his skin.

I opened my eyes and stared at the stove without seeing it. I had no wish to commit blasphemy, but surely John the Apostle knew that he spoke to the flesh. I remembered myself as a girl at a dance, tracing the flower pattern that trailed across my own young John's fancy vest. I had followed my fingers until they touched his belt, then pressed my whole hand flat to the silk. I remembered Martha Moody's dress wet against her hips.

I jumped up when I heard him in the yard, calling goodbye to his friends. I put my copying in my sewing chest under the merino and shovelled more coal into the stove. The fire had barely caught when he walked in the door.

John's brass horn glinted in the lamplight. He set it on the table and stooped to take off his boots. I saw goose-bumps rise on the stretch of pink skin above his socks. John hugged himself and went to stand next to the stove. I opened the damper to let more air into the fire.

"Why is it so cold in here?" John dipped his hands in the pot of water that sat on the stove. "This water is barely warm." He flicked his fingers at me. Water sprinkled my face. I didn't like it, but I laughed. I was still stirred from my reverie, and pushed myself to be amiable.

John found the towel and washed his face and hands. His skin was so fair that he blistered if he stepped outside without a hat. He liked to keep clean. His cheeks glowed as he looked at me, waiting for an answer.

"I was drowsing over my Bible." I rubbed the water from my face with my sleeve and tried to please him with flattery. "You look so like an angel tonight, with your flaxen hair and your trumpet."

John pushed the towel in my face with his whole hand, covering my eyes. I stood there stock still without moving or protesting, mindful of his sudden temper and a little afraid. When he took his hand away, he was striking a pose, with his horn clasped to his chest, his blue eyes lifted to heaven and his bee-stung lips making a small circle of awe. I took a deep breath of relief, then I laughed again and clapped my hands.

"Hallelujah." The coals hissed, finally giving out heat. I closed the door of the stove and watched him take off his shirt. "Good practice with the band?" I took his shirt from him and went to our bedroom. If I were tidy, he might come to bed happy.

I could hear him checking windows, putting chairs in their proper places, turning out the lamp. He didn't answer my question, but sang softly and sweetly, "Lord of our fa-ah-thers, ruler of all na-a-tions . . ."

I smiled and unlaced my corset. I stood for a moment with my nightgown in my hand, the cold air on my skin. I pulled the gown over my head before John came into the room. He carried a candle, and his head cast a shadow like a halo on the ceiling.

John and I didn't touch often. He was an elegant man, and liked the feel of clean, ironed sheets more than he cared about rubbing himself across my body's mounds. I understood his happiness to be standing in the road on a moonlit night, playing under a friend's window with his fellows, moving his foot in time inside his boot, and finding harmony and rhythms with the rest of the band.

Now I watched him comb his thinning hair before he came to bed. I knew he found me slatternly because my body flopped under my nightgown, and because I let dust settle in the house for weeks. But I had read my Bible, and knew that, of Martha who worked hard in her house and Mary who sat at the Lord's feet, Jesus said that Mary had chosen the better part. I wanted the life of the mind and the salvation of my soul, and I wanted the embrace of my husband that night.

John crawled into bed beside me. I waited. If he would reach over and run his hands against my breasts, it would be simple. John patted my hand and turned on his side, facing away from me. I moved my leg so it touched the curve of his buttocks. He seemed unnaturally still. I was tight to the snapping point, my whole body pulled rigid with unwomanly desire. I rocked my hips a little, so my leg brushed against him, moved away, brushed again. I felt wanton and aggressive, but I didn't stop.

John smelled like soap and cork grease. His neck had burned red in the weak sun. His feet were cold when I found them with mine. I spoke. "May I warm those up for you?"

"I guess." John started breathing steadily, a man who sounded asleep. I stopped moving, and wondered if I could sleep myself, or if I should get up and read my Roman history or the *Life of Martha Washington.* It was cold outside the blankets. I didn't rise, and I could not rest. I lay on my back watching the flickers cast on the ceiling by the light from the stove and listening to John breathing. I started moving my legs again, this time rubbing them against each other. I thought I would go crazy. I crawled around on the bed, trying both to wake John and to act like a quiet wife, until I had my face at the foot of the bed. I folded back the comforter so I could stick my head out and breathe, careful not to make a draft on his feet. I took one foot between my hands and started rubbing to warm it. I barely had time to feel the chill between my palms before he pulled his foot away and pushed my nightgown up over my hips. He was inside me quickly, and I was angry, angry, angry as he pumped at me. He had managed to find me drawn and dry, so there was no pleasure for me in his act. I shoved my hips back against him, and it must have hurt, because he dropped his full weight on my back to keep me still. He spent his seed, and lay on me for a moment before he turned away to sleep, but that moment under him with my wish for his body fulfilled and my breath pressed out of me was long enough for me to frame a suitable sentiment: "Lord, by this time he stinketh."

Two

The next morning I milked Miss Alice with more motion than John found decent. He had mentioned it to me before. He didn't like the way my body shifted with the rhythms of my hands. I had big hips and a belly that folded back against me when I leaned to reach Miss Alice's udders, but I was small compared to Martha Moody. John was still sleeping, so I sat in my loose dress on my short stool and told Miss Alice a story about a woman named Ida as we worked.

Ida was married to a farmer down in Oklahoma and gave birth to seven children. The day the youngest started walking, she took all of their savings, three hundred dollars, and bought a house in Stillwater. She said the children needed a city place. She didn't tell her husband, whose money it was by law and custom, until she had the children all packed and dressed and ready to go for the first stay in a town with a library. They had a furious fight. Ida and the children fled in the wagon. When they came back in two weeks, with storebought oranges, Ida found her husband dead on the kitchen floor, with a shotgun way across the room or right next to the body, depending on whether you rely on family memory or the local newspaper accounts. Her children did grow up knowing how to act in town, but Ida got strange. She stayed out on the farm, afraid of being poisoned, and it got so that the only time she left the house was to go to the barn to do the milking and watch the milk go from the cow to the bucket with her own eyes, and drink it quick before there was any chance of wrong-doing. She stood the local authorities off with a shotgun for as long as she could, but they were bound and determined to put a lake over her house for the town water supply, so they finally tied her into her own rocking chair and carried her, bitter and mean, to her daughter's place in Stillwater, where she lived more years than she cared to, then died. By the time the bucket was full and I had finished talking, I had a plan.

I made John bacon with corn fritters for breakfast. When he had finished and gone, I picked up his plate and used my finger to write my name in the grease. Then I put a block of my best butter in a flowered bowl, covered it with a clean dishrag, and took the road to town.

Clay Spencer yelled hello from his back pasture where he was wiping his face with a yellow handkerchief while his other arm was wrapped around the neck of his mule. I waved my arm. "Tell Clara I'll be by later."

When I got to Moody's Store, I stopped on the porch to shake the dust from the hem of my skirt. The green-striped awning read "CIGARS * CANDY * NOTIONS * M. Moody, Prop." Martha had painted "STAPLES AND FANCY GROCERIES" on the side of the store in big red letters edged with black. Brass bells tinkled when I pushed open the door, and Martha stood behind the pine counter, unpacking magazines from a box.

She looked up. "Morning, Mrs. Linger," she said, wiping her hands on her black ruffled apron. She looked large and perfect, as if she had been born tending the store. Her silk sleeves rasped against the counter as she pushed the glass jar of peppermints closer to the front edge, then she folded her hands in front of her, ready to wait on me.

I nodded before walking quickly to the back of the store where the fabric and notions were kept. Behind the counter, she looked prosperous and shaped like a vault. I couldn't imagine what I had already seen: Martha in the water with her calves soft and wet in the air. That vision had carried me all the way to town, but now it sunk in a rising sense of myself as a shabby wife from a one-cow farm. My butter was still in its bowl, half-hidden under my shawl. I touched the satins and cottons, and pulled a foot of gold fringe from its spool, then rolled it up again. The brass bells jangled, and the sheriff came in to ask Martha about a belt buckle he'd ordered. I set the bowl down on a shelf and dug through a basket of thimbles, listening to her firm voice and his soft one. The sheriff paid for his buckle and a sack of peppermints, and still I stood in the back with the bolts of cloth, hot with shame because I had come here with an idea.

I could hear Martha's dress rustling as she moved behind the counter. I thought she would come to me with her scissors and measuring tape—then I could talk to her from a natural distance, instead of across that wide counter—but she didn't come, and the bells rang again.

It was Theda Wilks in a poplin dress, and she was buying a chopping tool. She hefted everything from mauls and hatchets to ice picks, and settled on an axe with a blue handle that she tossed from hand to hand.

"Hello, Amanda," she called, taking a broad swing and slicing the air. "Shall I cut a length of silk for you, to test the blade?" I knew Theda from church suppers and temperance meetings, where she always presided. I had also seen her from a distance astride a horse, wearing bright green velveteen chaps. She was closer to my friend Clara than she was to me, but I knew why she wanted the axe. Every woman in town knew, and most men suspected. I tried to speak, but my tongue had turned to cloth.

"Sharpness guaranteed, or I'll grind it again myself." Martha's voice was law and order, and Theda stopped swinging the axe.

She strode over to the counter and opened her purse. "Did you know that Mrs. Carry A. Nation will be in town tomorrow, Martha?"

Martha rang up the purchase. "I've seen the notices."

I picked up my bowl and a package of pins, then walked to the front of the store and stood in line behind Theda. Her elegance from the back gave me nerve. "It's a great thing," I said, "to have her coming to lead us in battle against demon rum."

"Amen, sister." Theda nodded, but kept her eyes on Martha. "Will you be coming to hear her speak, Mrs. Moody?"

Martha stacked her change neatly on the counter. "I don't believe in demons, or vandalism, either."

Theda took the coins in her white fingers and turned to go. She said, "I'll pray for you, Mrs. Moody," and reached out to tap me on the forehead with the flat side of her axe. "See you tomorrow, Amanda."

Martha shook her head as she rang up my pins. "Wanton lawlessness, the way that Carry Nation breaks up saloons."

I was a teetotaller, but I didn't want to talk abstinence. I raised my bowl and pulled the dishrag off with a flourish. The butter was pale yellow and sweating a little, smooth and blank and whole in the bottom of the bowl. I held it out to her, and said, "Could I supply you with butter?"

I wanted to make my own money. I wanted to see more of Martha. Miss Alice gave milk that churned up sweet, and I was patient and attentive to the rising cream.

Martha took the bowl from my hands and set it down on the counter. Without saying a word, she walked down the aisle and came back with a knife and a loaf of bread. She stood next to the cash register and cut a thick slice, then slid the knife into my softened butter and spread it on the bread. She closed her eyes and took a bite. I watched her taste my wares. She nodded her head. "It's good. Can you bring it in quarter-pound balls?" She opened her eyes.

"Yes." There were gold crumbs on her breasts.

She offered me fifty cents a pound, a very good price, then she cut a slice from the loaf for me. I held it in my hand while she leaned across the counter with the butter knife. She made a slow swipe across the bread, then her knife slipped, and she buttered my wrist.

I stood in the road and licked the slick spot after I walked out of Moody's store. I had left the rest of the butter with her.

When I opened the door to my house, Clara Spencer backed out of my pantry with a jar of last year's pickles in her hand.

"Hello, Amanda," she said, rubbing dust from the jar with her puffed sleeve. "I was just admiring your mastery of the domestic arts."

I put my empty bowl on the table. "You probably wanted to see how thick the dust was, Clara, but I would have thought you'd have more interesting things to stick your head in, like our sheets."

Clara sat down at the table, untying her bonnet. "Oh, are those interesting? That's new." I gave her a swat with my shawl, and we both laughed.

Clara was recklessly curious, and a gossip as well, but if I hadn't been neighbors with her, I would have been one of the shy farm wives in back corners at church socials. She towed me through the midst of Ladies Committee Meetings, chatting indiscriminately. Theda Wilks would rustle up to Clara to discuss the subscription drive to bring Mrs. Carry A. Nation to Moody, and I could hold my ground against the impact of Theda's hourglass figure in peacock-blue watersilk when I was standing next to Clara, who wore valentine lace. Clara was tiny and went for the human rosebud effect. She decorated idle conversation with teeth pulling, mule trading, one-eyed babies and affairs of the heart. Theda and the other ladies would lean close to hear her, and Clara would clutch my arm and ask what I knew about the progress of gangrene. She was the reason the town ladies knew me more than just to nod to, and if they asked me to serve lemonade at an occasion, I felt at home enough to move the table out so I wouldn't spill all the glasses with my hips. I never had elegance, but I had common sense.

She ran down the hill behind the back of her house and crossed the field to see me almost every day. Today she had brought me a batch of gingerbread and the latest issue of *The Smasher's Mail.*

"It's not just alcohol, you know. Mrs. Nation hates tobacco, the Masonic Lodge, high fashion, and the Republican party, too. Read the editorial." Clara licked gingerbread from her fingers. She had small hands, and her sleeves were trimmed with green satin ribbon.

I poured each of us a glass of milk, and sat down. "I hear she's a powerful speaker. Do you think she'll inspire us tomorrow to clean out that vipers' pit?" John abstained, but I had known plenty of men who frequented bars when I was a single woman working at a boarding house. I didn't exactly think of them as vipers, but I loved the way the phrase rolled off my tongue.

"Praise Jesus, we'll do his will." Clara stood up, too excited to sit still. "Just bring something to smash with."

She wandered around the room, glancing at the dishes I'd left unwashed from John's breakfast, standing a minute at the front door to look over the garden towards the barn.

I picked up the paper and read aloud. "'Sister Carry is never diverted from her divine mission of urging Christian women to rise up against the purveyors of Satan's broth.' Newsprint came off on my fingers. "She's a woman of firm purpose."

"I can't wait," said Clara, opening my sewing chest. "How are you coming with this?" She unfolded my maroon merino, and the sheets of copied Bible verse fell out onto the floor.

She picked them up and scanned them before I could get out of my chair. "Oh, the story of Lazarus," she said. "Words of hope."

I was about to snatch the pages out of her hands, when she folded them with the merino and put it back in the chest.

She picked up the tape measure. "Amanda, do you think I need rubber hips? I saw an ad in the back of *Harper's Bazaar.* You can order them with dimples and all."

I was irritated, but willing to talk about anything except why I had hidden in my sewing chest the story of Mary wiping Christ's feet with her hair. I counted on Clara being less interested in piety than in falls from grace. "You have perfectly good hips."

Clara turned to me with the measure. "But they're nothing like yours. Can I measure you, Amanda? I might make you a petticoat. I have an extra length of lace."

I raised my arms and let Clara measure my widest parts. She would pester me endlessly if I kept her from something she wanted to know. I didn't feel judged, just mapped. She knelt on the floor in front of me to get the length from my waist to my ankles, writing down my dimensions on the margins of *The Smasher's Mail.* When she wrapped the tape around me from buttocks to paunch, she said, "That I can have no more children is my great grief."

Clara had spoken of this before. She had lost two babies days after they were born, and the doctor said she would have no more. "Clay is reconciled to the loss," she said, pulling the tape tight. "We do still touch."

John and I were also childless, but it was something quiet between us, almost agreed upon. I controlled our sex as best I could, so we kept to two weeks after my bleeding, when I thought the egg must be gone. I must have been lucky or barren by nature, because the bleeding always came. Children were wonders to me, and I found them good company, but I never felt solid enough to be a mother.

I looked down at Clara's face, and watched it swell and tighten like bread in the oven as she wrote down the width of my hips.

Clara said no more as she got up to chart my small bosom and my thick waist. It was common for us to veer into harsh subjects, then back to the quality of Miss Alice's cream, then onto the preacher's missing fingers, until we had drawn a sketch of most of our worlds. I told Clara about my new butter business, but I said nothing about Martha in the water or the flat of her knife on my wrist.

I was walking Clara to the back gate when we heard the music. It was early in the day, but the band must have called an extra practice so that they could perform after Mrs. Nation's lecture the next day. Theda Wilks had not invited them, but they would be ready to play, nonetheless.

I had told John they had to practice in the barn because of their spit valves and tobacco, but it was the music as much as the mess. They always played the same few songs—hymns and marches intended to stir the Temperance Army on the path to higher glory, but the music separated me from my thoughts. John's horn by itself had a light, sweet sound, but with the band he was as somber as the others.

Clara stopped, cradling the pitcher of cream I had given her, and looked towards the barn. "Do you ever go listen?"

"I have to listen whether I want to or not, but if I actually walk down there they stop playing and wait for me to go." I wrapped my shawl around me more tightly and shrugged. "It's for men."

Clara was already cutting across the garden to the barn. She turned back to me and said, "Just to see."

The big door of the barn was propped open with an oat bucket. We peered around the edge of it. I could see my husband John standing next to the ladder to the hayloft, shoulders hunched over his horn. The other men were playing and nodding and thumping their feet. The Reverend had his cheeks pouched out blowing his trombone. Only Miss Alice looked up at us from her stall.

> *Blessed be the ties that bind*
> *Our hearts in Christian love.*

Watching John sway in his music made me remember the elegance that had drawn me to him in the first place. I had been working in a boarding house in Moody, serving meals for a big table full of men. I carried the trays raised high over my head so I could turn sideways behind their chairs to put the food on the table. The men leaned over platters of chicken and long gravy boats, sopping grease with their biscuits and talking loudly about farms, mines, prospects, and the best routes farther west. Mrs. Luz, the owner of the boarding house, and I made three meals a day for nineteen, plus providing clean dishes, floors and linens. I went to sleep exhausted and dreamed long dreams of water closing over my head.

Mrs. Luz believed that cooks should eat before they started feeding everyone else. She and I sat in the kitchen one very early morning for our private meal. She had made us an omelet with chilies and pork left from supper the night before, and a sweet pudding.

"You have nothing to worry about." She rested her elbows on the bare wood table and took a long, slow drink of milk. "You're a big girl. You've got the hips for babies. The men will want you." She licked white foam from her lips. "You go to the dance."

I took a bite of egg. "There are too many men who want a woman to work for them, bring them their shoes in the morning, wash their feet for them at night. I see it in boarders all the time."

Mrs. Luz picked up a piece of melon. She scraped the rind with her teeth and juice spilled onto her fingers. "Go on to the dance tonight. I'll do the supper dishes. A young girl should be delicious, not think about the work of her life. You work hard enough already. You think one man would be worse than all these sitting around the table, out of bread, out of coffee, out of meat?"

I liked sitting in the kitchen in the early morning, eating something fresh and getting advice from Mrs. Luz. I imagined I could own a boarding house and save enough to hire girls to cook for me. I imagined marrying a tailor who would sew me upper skirts looped with bows of blue ribbons and a headdress of green chenille with satin beads. I was silly in the morning before we had to fire up the big oven and start the baking for the rest of the day.

My parents had both died of influenza when I was three. I had been raised by an aunt and had come west to hire out as soon as I could save up the money for my passage. I was plain and had no family to back me, but I didn't care once the music started on a Saturday night. There were few enough girls in Moody that I could have a partner whenever I wanted one.

Most of the men were lead-footed and eager to marry, but I danced between chairs and walls and tables all day with platters full of hot food, so I was light on my feet and fearless enough to move my big hips. People backed off. I cleared space for my partner and me on the crowded floor.

John was a fine dancer. I used to love to move in his arms. We always danced at the front of the hall, and he called out to the band members over my shoulder. He would bring three white shirts to a dance, so he could take off a damp one and be fresh again as the evening wore on.

Later, when Mrs. Luz was dead and I was married to John, sitting by the fire mending his shirts while he played in the barn, I wondered how I had understood music as a thing to let me move. I had lost all sense of that. John and I worked like two mules, and the best dream I could come up with over John's half-sewn shirts was to be another animal, a cow as beloved as Miss Alice, grazing when she wanted, fed in the winter, combed and milked and held in high regard. She bawled when we took her calf to be slaughtered, but that seemed like a brief trouble in a long life.

Miss Alice pushed her nose into my skirt, looking for grain. She had walked out to me and Clara as the men played on. I danced backwards a couple of steps over the bumpy ground. Our shadows were enormous, spreading halfway up the side of the barn. Clara was pressing her cheek to the splintery door, staring as the men's hands fluttered on the valves of their horns. I whispered in her ear. "Would you care to dance?"

Clara pointed at her shoes and shook her head, so I bowed to Miss Alice, then waltzed across her shadow, watching my wide outline darken hers, then I spun my skirts out over the cropped grass. Miss Alice followed me. I spun again and again. When I stopped, I felt Miss Alice's breath on my arm, and Clara made silent clapping motions with her hands.

Three

Carry A. Nation breezed into town the next afternoon. I took the garden shovel from the shed and walked down to meet the train, stepping lightly. I had changed into my old purple calico.

I stopped to hit the shovel against the Reverend's picket fence and knock the clumps of dried mud from its blade, then I twirled it over my head like a parasol. Dirt rained down my back, but I didn't care.

I passed Martha Moody, who was sitting at a table under the awning outside her store, sipping from a goblet and selling hatchets tied with white ribbon bows. Clara told me later that Martha had been drinking water. She claimed to have walked up to chat and sniffed the goblet. Clara had run up quite a bill at Moody's and couldn't afford to speak ill of the proprietress, but she couldn't stand not having a story to tell.

Martha and I nodded to each other. I raised my eyebrows at her, holding the shovel genteelly under my arm. "Encouraging vandalism?"

She took a sip from her goblet. "Just doing business."

Carry Nation was saying, "Satan, Satan, Satan" as I reached the crowd. The good women of the town were standing in the road outside the station. Even the most fashionable were wearing sturdy skirts and holding tools. I saw at least ten of

Martha's hatchets. The Oddfellows Brass Band was clumped with the rest of the men across the street in front of the bank. I caught a glimpse of John's pink-and-gold head as he leaned down to talk to the sheriff, who was short and wore a lace handkerchief tucked in his hat band. I spotted Clara's arm in dotted swiss, waving a hoe, and went to stand beside her.

Mrs. Nation was speaking from the platform, a small woman with a puffy face and round glasses. Elegant Mrs. Theda Wilks stood slightly behind her, holding a tambourine and her axe. Mrs. Nation had a small silver hatchet tucked at her waist, and her voice was as persuasive as potato wine.

"Liquor," she said, "liquor is Satan's broth. It burns the throat, it wrecks the home, it bloats the heart—soaks it and bloats it until there is no room in the drunkard's bosom for family love or compassion, honor or duty or piety, not one inch of his higher nature that hasn't been leached and rotted with drippings from the devil's cup." Her body was shaking and her fingers were clenched. Theda Wilks hit the tambourine one sharp, jangling rap.

Mrs. Nation bent towards us. "We've seen," she whispered. "Women see the bleakness. We see the strain on the face of the lost. We put tin forks on the table and wait for a mouth alive enough to eat our meals. *We* are the drunkards, whether or not we once take a drink." We listened to her, quiet, leaning on our weapons. The men across the street were stirring, murmuring to each other, looking at their watches.

I wasn't sure she was making sense, but I listened. Clara's face was rapt. Mrs. Nation raised her voice. "We have sight and we have power, God's power, the power Jesus gives us to face the sons of Satan in their den. Smash the bottles, smash the demon. Jesus has given us our charge. Are you ready? Smash, women, smash!"

Theda Wilks set a rhythm, hitting her axe against her tambourine. All of us caught it. We chanted. Clara was beating the handle of her hoe against the ground. The sheriff was trying to make his way to the platform, but ladies were packed tight around him, and he didn't want to shove.

Clara put her arm around my waist. "Smash," she said softly. "Smash."

"Jesus!" Mrs. Nation stopped to give us a slow, flat look, then began to quote the Bible. "We are compassed about with a great cloud of witnesses, prophets and martyrs, 'who through faith subdued kingdoms, wrought righteousness, obtained promises, stopped the mouths of lions, quenched the violence of fire, escaped the edge of the sword, out of weakness were made strong, waxed valiant in fight, turned to flight the armies of the aliens.'"

"Evil rum!" Clara shouted. "Demon rum!"

"Amen, sister." Theda Wilks dropped her tambourine and raised her axe in both hands to the sky.

"'They were stoned.'" Mrs. Nation's bonnet had slipped back, so her grey hair showed. Her voice was heating up. "'They were sawn asunder, were tempted, were slain with the sword: they wandered about in sheepskins and goatskins; being destitute, afflicted, tormented'!"

Women were turning all around us. Mrs. Nation ran from the platform, her silver hatchet in her hand, screaming, "Smash, smash, for Jesus' sake, smash!" Theda Wilks jumped down behind her, yellow skirt flying. Then we were all running, running for the saloon with its gilt sign and its swinging doors.

We must have passed the men, and Martha, too, if she hadn't gone inside and bolted her door, but all I saw was Clara's dotted swiss in front of me, darkening with sweat as she ran. Theda Wilks kicked open the door and we surged into the empty saloon.

Clara pulled me towards the bar, but I stopped cold. She left me. I stood in a corner that smelled of fried potatoes and sweat, not able to take one more step with my sisters in Christ, who were leaping into the fray.

I watched my friend Clara, who flirted in church, splinter a chair with her hoe. She kept hacking at the seat, as if Satan himself were sitting there.

Carry Nation swung her hatchet with intensity, but I didn't see her smashing the devil or her husband or anything that wasn't there. Mrs. Nation went after the bottles themselves, frantic to get at the liquid. As dark streams began cutting across the floor, she knelt in the sawdust and washed her hands. I saw her look up at her reflection in the big mirror over the bar and tap the lenses of her glasses as if to get at the liquid balls behind them. She must have felt me staring, because she raised her small arms and heaved her hatchet at the mirror, screaming, "Smash, smash, smash, smash!" Clara and Theda Wilks ran back and forth behind her, snatching bottles by their long necks and bursting them into shards on the railing.

I shrank against the wall, crying and hugging my shovel. I saw the men gathering outside the door, urging the sheriff forward. The women ripped the liquor case from the wall, and it crashed with a roar like the voice of Judgment.

I was stupid with shaking. I hadn't broken one goblet. I could do nothing with the shovel but hug it like a baby.

All the others were shouting. Theda Wilks stood on the bar and raked her axe across a painting of a naked woman. "Virtue!" she screamed as the canvas ripped. She unhooked the painting from the wall and flung it to the floor.

Outside, I heard John's band strike up, "What a Friend We Have in Jesus," and I knew I had to get out of that room.

Mrs. Nation, looking drained, leaned against a table. Theda Wilks brought her a chair, and Mrs. Nation sank into it. She grasped Theda's hand.

"Praise Jesus," said Theda. "Praise the Lord for bringing you into our midst."

"You are kind to a stranger." They both started sobbing. The women gathered around them. I bent and picked up one of the green bottles that had landed whole near my feet. I hid it beneath my cloak.

Clara stared in surprise. She had seen.

God, how I hated myself at that moment, with Clara's eyes meeting mine across the sobbing backs of principled women. I had prayed with them. I had eaten Clara's three-bean casserole and Theda's German chocolate cake. Now Clara turned away in the half-light, and I knew myself to be a coward and a common thief. As suits a thief, I slipped out the back as the sheriff burst through the front with the saloon-keeper and the husbands close behind him.

I ran down the alley, past the back doors of Moody. Mrs. Nation was shouting something about Caesar. Blasts from John's band followed me as if I were waiting by the stove at home. They were playing "Onward, Christian Soldiers," in support of the good fight. My arms were heavy, and I had dropped the shovel, but still held the bottle of wine under my cloak. It

Susan Stinson

bounced against my hip as I ran. My face was dripping sweat, my hem was damp with spirits, my mouth was full of spit. I felt flooded.

I wished Mrs. Luz were still alive, so I could bring her a gift of wine and wash up in her private bath. As I ran and stumbled, I could hear her husky voice giving me scientific instruction in the domestic arts: "All beverages contain a large percentage of water, and serve to quench thirst, to introduce water into the system and regulate the temperature; to carry off waste; to nourish; to stimulate the nervous system and various organs."

The smell of whiskey rose to me in waves. My skirt was drenched in the stuff. I hugged the wine bottle and wondered if Mrs. Luz would intervene in heaven for me to turn the wine back to water. I decided that I needed the water cure. I should keep running along the back ways and fields to home, where I would soak sheets for sweating, take a plunge bath in the tub, then drink twenty glasses of water and wrap wet bandages around my neck, chest, and abdomen. I would bury the bottle somewhere discreet.

Instead, when I saw the low fence that marked Martha Moody's back yard, I hoisted my skirts and jumped it. I landed on my feet in her vegetable patch. I didn't know if she would offer me shelter, but I walked up to her back door and knocked.

I heard a brisk step, then Martha opened the door. She was wearing a blouse and skirt, and her hair was pulled smooth. Dusk was falling, and I was losing myself with the light. She stood out more boldly, outlined from behind by the hall lamp.

"I need help," I said, remembering her throwing herself over rocks in the stream. I pulled the bottle out from under my cloak and waved it at her.

She put her hand on my shoulder and drew me in.

Warmth from the kitchen stove washed over me as I stopped on the doormat to take off my shoes. They stank in my face as I unlaced them, soaked with whiskey and beer. Martha watched me shivering over my wet feet, then motioned me to the table.

I sat in a straight-backed chair and put the bottle of wine down in the middle of her linen tablecloth.

Martha ignored it, reaching under the sink to bring out a porcelain basin. She set it on the floor next to my chair, then picked up the kettle and poured steaming water into the basin. "For your feet," she said. "They are wet and cold."

I watched painted flowers on the bottom as they wavered under the water. "And they smell like a still."

Martha knelt on the floor next to me, her back rippling under the fabric of her blouse. I looked down at my own lap and followed the weave of the calico, as if each stitch meant something, then I gathered the hem of my dress about my knees. Martha reached up to unclip the top of my stocking. She rolled it down. My leg was shining everyplace she touched. She lifted my foot into the water.

It was warm. She rubbed her fingertips against my sole, making little circles at the hard places. I had a flicker of embarrassment at my callouses, but she held my foot between both palms as if it were butter she was trying to imprint with the shape of her hands. I felt like something precious. Martha washed and rubbed my other foot, then she unbuttoned her blouse and wrapped it around my feet to dry them.

I leaned down and touched the soft flesh folding over her shoulder blades. It moved like skin over water. Her flesh spilled out of the edges of her corset wherever it could. Bible verses were washing through my mind along with Mrs. Luz's recipe for making soap, as I watched Martha sit up to unlace her corset. I couldn't tell where her breasts stopped and her thighs began. Everything swelled and folded. As she loosened her laces and her belly rose, I had to look away.

I was afraid, but Martha was on her knees now, leaning across the basin to run her hands over the tops of my thighs. Every time she shifted, her breasts pressed into my lap.

I wrapped one leg around her to draw her to me. Martha knocked into the basin. Water spilled over her skirt and across the wooden floor. She pushed my skirt above my hips, and ran her fingers under the edges of my undergarments. Her knuckles pressed through the cloth where my legs parted, pressed and rubbed and pressed again. I was pushing against her, crying, not thinking, sliding off the chair with my crotch going over the tips of her breasts, over her belly, slipping down to her thigh where she held me, rocking back and forth, holding my hips down with both hands as I joined her motion. I was pulsing tighter and tighter when she pushed her finger inside me and rocked me against her thumb. Then I was lost to the senses, lost to motion, gone to the milky heart of the world where I churned and churned and churned.

After a time, I touched her neck. We went to bed. When she knelt above me, her belly lapped across my body. I was covered and sated and safe.

Four

When I woke in the morning, she had already opened the store. I sat up and drank three glasses of water, one after the other, listening to the brass bells jingling and Martha murmuring to customers. She had a big volume of Shakespeare next to the bed, and I ran my hands over the scratched leather cover without opening the book. Finally I got up and took a sponge bath, then got dressed. I found my shoes on the windowsill, considerably aired out.

I went downstairs when the store was empty and said goodbye to Martha. She came around the counter, packed and laced again into her formidable public figure. I pushed both hands into a barrel of dried beans past the wrists. We kissed. Then the bells jangled, and a man came to ask Martha about rope, so I extracted myself, and left. I had no idea what to say to John.

Our house was silent when I opened the door. I hurried into the bedroom to change out of my dress. It still reeked of liquor, but when I put my hands to my face, they smelled of Martha's soap. Mrs. Luz's household instructions floated into my mind again: Fats that are not fit for food may be made into soap.

Five pounds lukewarm melted fat, one can lye, one quart borax, two tablespoons vinegar, one teaspoon salt. Martha must have added almond extract to hers. It smelled sweet.

The bed was neatly made, and it occurred to me to wonder whether John had slept here himself last night, and where he might have been if he hadn't. Every thought I had was interrupted by flashes of Martha's wet hands on my legs, of Clara and Theda pulling down the rack of bottles with a crash, of the wild feeling that had welled in me when Mrs. Nation called the crowd of women out to battle.

I tried to quiet my mind with the task of wrapping the calico in an old sheet and setting it to soak in a bucket. I felt the cold bottle of wine in my fingers again, and felt Clara's stare across the wrecked saloon. I put on my grey skirt and white blouse, and went into the other room.

John's Sunday coat was folded over the back of the chair by the stove. I picked it up and saw that one sleeve was ripped off. The back of the coat was covered with dust. He had worn it yesterday to play with the band, and I couldn't imagine what he had done to come home in such a state. I felt Martha's soft belly brushing across me again, and was washed with such a flood of fear that I had to hold onto the table to steady myself. I heard Miss Alice bawling from the barn, and realized that I had missed two milkings. I hurried outside. I had spent the night drenching myself, but had neglected to give Miss Alice fresh water. I pushed open the heavy barn door.

John was sitting on my stool, milking a nervous Miss Alice. He had one hand on her neck to steady her, as she blew hard through her nose. She bawled again when she saw me, and John looked over his shoulder.

His eyes were red-rimmed and I could see that his hands were shaky on her teats. For a moment I believed that John had been on a drinking spree, then I realized that he had been crying.

He didn't get up. "Where have you been?"

I walked over to him and touched his shoulder, as if he were Miss Alice, to calm him. If I wasn't willing to do that, I should have begged Martha to let me stay with her. "I was evading arrest. Did they come looking for me?"

John folded his hands in his lap. "I was the only one looking for you."

I watched Miss Alice shift her weight and thought of Martha's sweet grace in bed as he told me how he had gone to the jail with the other men, but I had not been there to bail out. He had asked Clara if she'd seen me, but she said she wasn't sure that I'd ever been in the saloon.

John looked at me. "I saw you busting through that door with the rest of them. I spent half the night looking for you. Why didn't you come home?"

I stepped back from him and tried to gauge his mood. I had expected him to threaten me or to offer me a cold face like I got when I didn't have a shirt starched when he wanted to go to town. We had always exchanged feelings on a small scale. The mention of Clara had given me an opening. "I stayed in the spare room of someone I don't want to name. A friend. It was without the knowledge of her husband, who isn't such a strong supporter of temperance as you are." I hoped John hadn't gone back up to the Spencers' after Clara had lied to him, since I was implying that she had given me refuge. "I'm so sorry to have caused you worry, but I was terrified of going to jail."

Though it was mid-morning, it was almost dark in the barn. I thought I heard a rat rustling when John suddenly slipped off the stool onto his knees. He was kneeling much too close to Miss Alice, but she had calmed and stood quietly. He rested his elbows on the stool and said, "Dear Lord, we ask forgiveness for Amanda in her selfishness and cowardice."

I saw his face working with the beginnings of anger, and realized how exhausted he must be for it to take so long for his temper to catch. I was tired, too. I sat down on a bale and bent my neck.

John was going on about sin and wives and Adam's rib, sounding like he had a throat full of hay. My fear had ebbed, but so had my alertness. I found my head bobbing and jerking like a sleeper in church. John was working repentance hard when I noticed his horn on the bale next to mine. I picked it up, hoping that having something in my hands would keep me awake until he got to forgiveness. If I had been thinking straight, I never would have picked up John's horn. I knew it was a holy thing. I was idly pushing the valves in and out when John grabbed my wrist. I thought to drop the horn, but with his other hand he held my fingers tight around the shaft. "Go on and play it," he said. "Offer something up to God."

He put the horn to my face, then took my lips between his fingers and shaped them around the mouthpiece. "Blow," he said, standing over me.

All I could think of was spit. I had had years of his mouth, but now I didn't want to taste him on the metal. My chest hurt, and I was trying not to shake, but he bent his face towards mine, so I pushed what breath I had into the horn. Nothing came out. Suddenly, I wanted it, wanted sound, not just pressure that led to nothing but a sour grin on my husband's face.

"I'm listening," he said, squatting down with his ear to the bell.

I took a deep breath and tried to blast him. The air came out of me with effort but silently. I tried again, took a breath like a wave and let it break out of my lips with what should have been a roar, but it hissed ineffectually around the mouthpiece. I tried again, pulling my lips tight as I'd seen John do, sucking in my cheeks, pushing so that John would know he wasn't the only one with air and sound. I blew until my lips turned grey. I never came close to reaching a note.

John was satisfied. He took the horn and wiped it on his sleeve, then raised it to his lips. He stood on the swept dirt and blew. My own mouth ached as I watched him. His fingers arched and fell. He played softly, then the sound sharpened. As the notes joined in rhythm and in air, they joined him to something else. He was playing towards belief. It was a high-vaulted music that drew my eyes up to watch the curved bell dip and sway, but then I looked back at my lap. I didn't want to listen to John's song anymore.

John played himself out, then told me, "Amen."

I stood and took the half-empty milk bucket away from Miss Alice. She bawled something like the sound that I had wanted to offer John's ear.

"I forgive you," said John. We embraced. His smell cut into me like needles of hay.

———

I lay down beside him, but I couldn't sleep that night. His arm along my back was a weight. I moved it as gently as I could so as not to wake him, took a blanket from the chest, and slipped out of the room.

I moved John's coat from my chair by the stove, wondering again how it came to be ripped and dirty. I sat down and opened my sewing box, but pulled out my paper and pen. I took the Bible from the table as if for solace, but instead of searching for a verse to copy, I found myself using it as a lapboard as I wrote a story from thin air:

One day an angel was walking down the Main Street of Moody. She saw a store, and entered. A fat red-headed woman stood behind the counter. She nodded at the angel, and the angel recognized her. "Are you Martha Moody?"

Martha rang up a purchase and nodded again. "What's your pleasure?"

The angel blinked her large yellow eyes, and said, "I am Azreal, and I need a favor."

Martha said, "I can't take any time off the store." Azreal stuck her muzzle in a barrel and picked up an apple. "Come on. It'll just take a few moments of your time."

Martha frowned. "Don't bite that apple unless you're going to buy it. Can it wait until after five o'clock?"

Azreal licked the apple with her long tongue, then put it back in the barrel.

"Hey," said Martha.

Azreal held up her hoof. "That will make it extra sweet for some lucky customer."

Martha looked skeptical, but as soon as the angel had wandered off, she found the very apple and took a bite. It tasted like honey would if it had a peel.

Azreal was back at five sharp. She lowered the awning while Martha locked up.

Martha was used to being asked for favors, but she was curious about this character. "What would you have me do?"

Azreal suddenly looked grander. "Your task is to come to a dry town and use your powers to make it wet and green."

Martha stared at the angel as the store fell away around them. A wind came up and blew the gray cloak off of Azreal to reveal her in her full glory as a winged cow. She was the color of fine butter, with deep yellow skin, broad yellow udders with veins in the pattern of lightning, yellow at the end of her tail, and the inside of her ears and around the eyelids yellow.

Martha saw that she was no longer standing, but floating on blue air thick as cream. Her black dress melted away from her, and she found herself in a short garment of a shimmering white fabric she did not recognize, with thin straps and a pattern of eyelet flowers over her breasts. Her body was loose underneath— her corset frothed off her into ticklish bubbles—and she was moving all over herself, like the sky cream she was riding.

"Look down," lowed Azreal. Martha saw a hilly, green country, very different from Moody, with trees in abundance and black roads and strange houses at regular intervals. "You must make it wet and green," quoth Azreal.

"But it's already green," said Martha, turning onto her side so that she could see the cow flying beside her. "So many trees."

"It's dry at the heart, "Azreal insisted.

So Martha stretched out on her stomach and floated looking down through the clear blue cream to the clusters of houses and odd vehicles. *Azreal watched over her shoulder and breathed grassy smells on her back.*

When they were close enough, Martha saw people—women, mostly, and small boys and girls—carrying brown bags, talking, gliding the streets in closed wagons. They looked like the people of Moody, just dressed funny and most of the women were thinner—but a smell rose from them and their houses. Martha didn't recognize it, but it bit into her nose and made her eyes water.

"Dry rot." Azreal flicked her tail, and the cream sky darkened. "Go on, Martha. They're desperate."

Martha wondered how to go about bringing them liquid. She could cry them a river, but she wasn't that moved. In fact, she felt indifferent to lives whose dryness made her itch even from this distance. "Why don't you do it?" she asked Azreal.

The cow stretched her wings. "That's not my role. I just make the cream."

Martha knew a thing or two about cream. She dipped a flesh-rippled arm in the thick sky she was floating in.

"So that's it. Okay. I'll churn the air."

"You can stand on my back if you want." Azreal beat her wings and flew close to Martha. "To have a solid surface."

So Martha climbed onto the back of the yellow angel cow. Azreal's back was broad, and Martha's feet were bare, so when she squatted for a moment, then stood up straight, she had a firm footing. She wanted to beat as much of the cream as she could, so she started swinging her arms and rolling her hips, the big swings of her belly moving the cream in a firm circle. Her hips stirred from the front and the back, and her arms caught the motion over her head and brought it back down to her hips again. She moved like sex, like magic, like the ocean she carried with her in her rippling back. The soft parts of her body that she couldn't agitate floated back and forth in rhythm as she worked. It was hypnotic and exhausting. Martha didn't learn so much motion in childhood, but grew into it with her breasts and the rolls of her sides. She walked forward on Azreal's back with her hips and arms rolling, then turned on her toes and walked to the tail. Azreal sang low repetitions in the ancient voice of Cow, to help.

They hung in froth that lasted for what seemed hours, a screen of small blue bubbles that clung to Azreal's hide and Martha's skin, but slid off her shiny slip. They could no longer see the town, but Martha had closed her eyes anyway, to concentrate. She forgot about the people, forgot about dryness, but lost herself in texture, in nuances of foam as it slipped down her sides, as it clung to her eyelids and coated her hair. She felt herself swelling, arms and belly spreading until she and Azreal could move the whole sky.

Then it happened. It thickened. Martha's breaths came slow and filtered through blue whipped cream. Azreal kept singing. Martha waved and rolled and danced. Quickly the cream clotted and buttermilk spilled upon the people who had been pursuing their business as if the sky were a far and placid place.

Martha sat on Azreal, who flapped her wings slowly to help her gather the butter into a ball.

"That's the moon," Azreal told her. "They'll see it shine tonight."

Martha dug some craters with her fingers. "Do you go through this every month?"

Azreal shook her head. "Not that often. But these people are so hollow that they suck the moon down to nothing. So I look for a woman with strength and succulence who can churn my cream to

*butter when it gets too bad. There's nothing like buttermilk rain
for dry rot."*

*Martha glanced down. It all looked about the same, only
glossy.*

Azreal landed. "Thank you so much."

*Before Martha could answer, she was standing at the counter
of her closed store, with an apple sweet as honey in her hand.*

I woke in the chair before dawn. The pad of paper, the Bible,
and John's coat were in a pile on the floor by my feet. I rubbed
my stiff neck. The jagged sound of John's breathing filled the
house, but it seemed to come from some far place. I picked
up the pad, and tore off the pages of my story. The shape of
Martha's name in my blue handwriting gave me a feeling of rest.
Azreal the winged cow made me shiver and laugh. I folded the
pages and stuck them into my sewing chest under the neglected
merino, then set the Bible in its place on the little table by the
stove.

By the time John came scratching and yawning into the
kitchen, I had made a breakfast of biscuits, sausage and eggs. I
put the milk pitcher on the table, but left John to pour his own
glass.

"Wife, this smells wonderful." John used my title at
intimate moments: when he left my body in satisfaction, when
I offered him a good meal. He really must have forgiven me
yesterday. He shoved eggs onto his fork with a biscuit.

I sipped my milk and watched him chew. His lips were
dappled with egg. He seemed simple, and I felt stirrings of

guilt for the complexities of my affections. I distracted myself.
"What happened to your coat?"

"Oh, that." John wiped his lips with a napkin, beaming.
"That was a fist fight. Some roughs outside the jail were speaking
ill of the sacrifice the ladies had made for temperance."

I lifted the damp glass for another gulp of milk. "I hope
no one was hurt."

John drank his coffee. "No, the Reverend stepped in." He
was looking at me expectantly, so I patted his hand.

"Sounds like quite a show of moral courage." The bones
of his wrist seemed large and odd and visible. I took my hand
away. "Perhaps we ladies were overzealous, John, but our
motives were pure." I was surprised at the thrill I felt saying
"moral," "overzealous" and "pure." The words buzzed a little as
they rolled off my lips. I had never been a petty liar, but now I
liked the subtle vibrations in my voice.

John's cheeks were stretched with egg. "Good might come
of it."

I could track each swallow down his skinny throat. My
enjoyment passed into a feeling like danger or nausea or urgency.
I stood up to clear the dishes and fill the sink. I put my hands in
water to the elbows, and said, "John, I'm going shopping today.
Do you need anything from Moody's store?"

John needed pipe tobacco. I walked the road to town wearing
my grey poplin for discretion with my satin bonnet for nerve. I
shuffled my feet in the dust, but kept up a good pace. When I
got to the Reverend's house on the edge of town, I bumped my

hip against each slat of his picket fence as I walked by. I wasn't wearing my corset.

This was only mildly reckless. I never wore the corset at home, except once when a lady photographer took our wedding picture. She couldn't come the day of the ceremony, so she rode out to our house three weeks later. I laced myself in, put on my veil, and took John's arm in front of the morning glories that trailed over the garden fence. John was prettier than me, with a big white bow tied up with flowers over his jacket pocket.

Most days, though, I needed my full range of motion for dumping the stove's ashes, tending the garden and hauling water to Miss Alice. The work bound me in other ways, but sometimes when I was pulling steaming white shirts out of the boiling washpot, I would get a jolt of pleasure from the clean path I was leaving in life. My work clothes were dark skirts and loose blouses, and I wore wool underclothes tight against my skin most seasons.

I usually laced myself in whenever I entered the social sphere of town, and sat through church being poked by stays, but my waist never approached slenderness. I didn't think I looked much different in the sturdy poplin without the corset, but I felt agile and immense. I took smooth steps, trying not to let my rear-end bounce beneath my skirt.

I was hurrying toward Martha with my shopping basket on my arm, too excited to think of what we'd say to each other when I got to her store in the middle of a business day. My mind distracted itself with the beginnings of a story that I wrote down that night. In it, Martha is a magic woman, huge past the point where size can be considered anything less than a blessing of range to the human world. She doesn't have to consider it at all. When she walks through the streets of town, her clothes stream off her, transformed into feathers, wings, colored sheets, strips of cloth, petals that fly off in a burst. She has majesty. Money sticks to the whorls of her fingers. She doesn't have to worry about anything.

I was so busy inventing Martha that I didn't notice Clara Spencer until I walked into her beneath the awning outside Moody's. She put her hand out to stop me from stepping on her shiny shoe, and I realized that she must have been standing there watching me come up the road.

She patted my arm with her small hand, and I shrunk back into my ordinary stature. "Amanda," she said, scanning my face, "I've been wondering how you are."

Her scrutiny made my chin tremble, but her voice was mild. Clara had seen me stealing spirits, but now as my eyes reddened, she tried to draw me gently into the store.

I pulled away. My face was puffy, and I was struggling not to cry. Clara looked hurt, but she tried again.

"Amanda, you can't cry on the public street. Come into the store. You were going shopping, too, weren't you? We'll buy what we came for, then we'll go someplace and talk."

I stared down at her skirt while I struggled for control. The last thing I wanted was to make a spectacle of myself outside of Moody's, but I didn't want to come to Martha crying with Clara on my arm. "Are you worried about Martha Moody?" Clara looked up the street to the train station, where a few women were clustered together near the platform, then back to me with her acute attention. "She might notice traces of emotion on your face, but Martha's not a gossip. She would never say a word."

I wiped my eyes and nodded, giving up. Clara opened the door. The brass bells rang. Martha came from the back and said, "Hello, Mrs. Spencer. Mrs. Linger." She didn't smile, but walked quickly behind the counter. Clara whispered, "What did I tell you? Discreet."

So I moved through the store, picking things up, putting them down. I hadn't come with any sort of list. Clara hurried to the dry goods. She looked through a stack of small mirrors, darting back to me to whisper a joke about the price of vanity. Martha turned to the shelves behind her, but I felt pulled by her silence, by the lines of her back under the stretch of black silk, by the ripples in her arms as she reached for a box, by the tight coil of her hair. I stopped at the counter, untying my bonnet as I spoke.

"Mrs. Moody, can you tell me where to find Old Prince tobacco?" My voice quivered. Clara gave me a worried glance.

Martha turned smoothly. "Yes, it's right here. Does your husband prefer a sack or a tin?"

Her voice was a cool burn. She had stretched it to say, "husband." I took off my bonnet and placed it on the counter. I thought that if I left it, I would have an excuse to come back later. I pushed it towards her. Clara was using two mirrors to check the state of her French twist.

I leaned across the counter to find Martha's hand, then held it and rubbed it over the curve of the bonnet.

"You." I said softly, but out loud.

Her palm slid open across the satin. Her face opened to show riches ready to drop upon me, like the sky in a poem she'd whispered in my ear the night before. I gestured that I wanted her to keep the bonnet, so she took it by its ribbons and hid it on a low shelf. "I was expecting butter this morning," she said under her breath.

She must have been waiting for me early, before the store opened. Clara walked over with some wide ribbon and a square mirror framed in black. "John likes a tin, does he not?"

She thought I didn't have the composure to answer Martha's question. Even in my confusion, I was touched. "That's right."

Martha rang our purchases up.

Clara took my arm and steered me behind the church to the cemetery. She said it was a quiet place to talk, but kept looking over her shoulder. My stomach was in knots. I had felt spark and venom in lying to John, but Clara knew the exact measurements of my hips, what Mrs. Luz had said to me on my wedding night, and that I remembered the shapes of my mother's hands as she had turned the pages of the Bible with me in her lap. She had a hankering for human facts, and might catch me in a lie. Besides, Clara was not my husband, but my friend.

We sat on a stone bench that the church Ladies' Committee had commissioned. My basket and her mirror rested between us. "We went to jail," she said. "Did you hear?"

"John told me." I looked at his tin of tobacco in the basket, and felt a twist of dislike.

"It was only a couple of hours before Clay came to get me. We sang hymns and prayed, but I was thinking about you."

"I didn't drink the wine," I said. I hadn't broken my pledge of abstinence anywhere but in my head.

"It doesn't matter," said Clara. "Jesus turned water into wine for his first miracle." She waved her hand. "I didn't tell anyone. God will forgive you."

Clara read six-month old magazines shipped in from the East instead of Gospel at night. She loved to be at the cutting edge of fashion, even of spiritual fashion, but she was telling me that she loved me more.

"Thank you, Clara." I hugged her. I dismissed the flash of worry that she would notice I wasn't wearing a corset, and let myself sink into relief without any further account of my fall from grace.

Clara held me tight for a moment, then drew back and straightened my collar for me, suddenly businesslike. She picked up her mirror, and said, "Come on. A few of us are gathering to see Mrs. Nation off, and I want you to make an appearance." She held up the mirror and flashed a reflection of my waist at me. "This is a gift for Mrs. Nation."

I tugged at the poplin and shook my head. "No, Clara, I can't face them," but she had already taken my arm. I let her drag me towards the station, chattering.

"As the men were taking us to the jail, I saw John get in a fist fight with a couple of drunken hooters. Last I saw of him, the Reverend had pulled him out of the dirt, and was holding on from behind to keep him from doing any more brawling. Both John and the Reverend were howling for God and justice, but no one paid them any mind in the general passion of the moment."

Clara tightened her hold on my arm. "John stopped shouting long enough to ask me if I'd seen you, but I said I hadn't."

"Thank you," I said, and meant it.

Clara plowed on. "Theda Wilks has been in her glory. She came to church this morning with her hatchet tucked in her belt. The Reverend wouldn't let her in the door."

"Speak of the devil." I spotted Theda Wilks as we neared the station. She was with a small group of the faithful on the platform, strutting nervously back and forth wearing a white sash emblazoned with "Faith, Hope and Charity." I had read in *The Smashers' Mail* that these were the names of Mrs. Nation's hatchets.

Mrs. Nation herself was facing the empty track with a black satchel in her hand. She looked small and respectable, although her hair was falling out of its knot. Theda walked over to Mrs. Nation and repaired her bun with a few decisive moves of the pins. Mrs. Nation nodded in thanks, then looked east again over the empty tracks.

"She's not going to address us," Clara told me. "She isn't feeling well. That's why there's so few of us to see her off. She doesn't want a fuss."

Firmly holding my arm, Clara stepped into the small group. The other women moved to embrace her with more emotion than usual. I supposed that the few hours in jail together had made a bond between them. They gave cordial nods to me. Clara had told me that others had escaped arrest by hiding or running down the alleys as I had, and no one thought worse of them for it. Still, as Theda Wilks strode over to us and enfolded Clara, I became very aware of my drab grey poplin and the loose movement of my body under my clothes. Theda was resplendent in bronze silk, but she barely had time to acknowledge me before Mrs. Nation beckoned her over.

"Come on," murmured Clara, hurrying after Theda to present Mrs. Nation with her mirror. She pulled me along with her.

Mrs. Nation took Clara's hand, then thrust the gift into her satchel without giving it a second glance. She was staring at me as intently as she had been staring up the tracks. I remembered the long look we had exchanged in the saloon when Mrs. Nation had tapped her glasses with her hatchet and I had decided that she was unbalanced. Now Mrs. Nation spoke in her resonant voice. "Who are you?"

I took a step backwards. Mrs. Nation's gaze was daunting, and all of the other women were looking at me, too. Clara squeezed my arm until I managed to say, "A Christian woman." It didn't occur to me to state my name.

Mrs. Nation's eyes slid over me. I felt her see that my body was not restrained under my dress. She made a hissing sound. "I think not."

Theda leaned down and spoke into Mrs. Nation's ear. I imagined her saying that I was no one. Clara opened her cupid's-bow mouth, but the train arrived with noise and smoke, so no one heard what she said. I stood with my arms crossed over my chest.

Theda hovered protectively as Mrs. Nation boarded the train with one quick wave for her sisters. Clara came back to my side, but I couldn't look at her.

The women spoke to me politely as Clara said her goodbyes, but they were reserved. Avoiding their eyes, I saw how the hair on each one's head shone like tassels of winter grass. It was a small field of women who heard what Mrs. Nation said to me. In the months ahead, I would feel them counting up the signs that it was true.

Five

I never went back for my bonnet, but I had a better reason to be with Martha. I sold her butter. All I had for cream was Miss Alice, so I couldn't make much, but I took care that what I made was sweet and fancy. I molded each half-pound lump into a perfect ball. I asked Clara, who was deft, to carve me an emblem. She whittled a stamp of a cream pitcher for me, and I pressed it into each ball before I wrapped it in white linen soaked in cold water. Martha displayed my butter in a glass case with ice. She paid me fifty cents a pound. I told John it was thirty.

He complained. "You barely make back what you spend on feed and linen."

John kept my accounts, since he said I was weak at adding, but I hiked up the costs so he thought I was earning almost nothing. His complaints weren't serious, since I had taken over the cost of feeding Miss Alice, and was doing all the milking, and he still had milk for coffee and biscuits in the morning. I kept the money in a tin can under a loose plank in Miss Alice's stall.

So I saw Martha three times a week when I brought in the butter. I got up before dawn to do the churning, then I carried it to her in a tub of ice. If I was fast, I could get out of the house without even seeing John, although I left the coffee brewing and biscuits warming in the oven.

Martha let me in the store as the light broke. She always kissed me once before she took the butter, but she was careful, almost reverent, in its care. She set it out on fresh ice in its glass display case before we went upstairs.

She had a big bed, with soft sheets and goosedown pillows. Watching her bend to fold a blanket made tears come to my eyes.

Martha never talked much, but I stroked her belly and told her Miss Alice's mood that morning, and what I'd said to Clara, and what I'd dreamed about the night before. If I asked her a question, she'd run her hands along my thighs with such smooth pulls that I'd be lost.

Sometimes she'd pick up the big leather Shakespeare that she kept on her bed table, and read me a sonnet about bare ruined choirs, or the expense of spirit in a waste of shame, or summer days. Her voice was deep and lovely, and I took the sentiments for her own.

She never asked me about John, and we never planned a future. I thought that neither one of us had spent much time happy, so we were giddy with an hour three times a week. I dressed simply those mornings because time was short.

I was surprised how much I knew about passion and discretion. I saved pints of cream for Clara for her pleasure over fruit, but I never spoke with her about Martha or the money in Miss Alice's stall. I fooled John with the books, and with wifely attentions. Although I hated our sex, it was rare. It was as if I had been going through my life dripping secrets, and had finally churned them to a thickness which was Martha.

John was in most nights now. Carry Nation's visit had spent Moody's temperance fever, and, like John, most of the horn players had gone back to their evenings at saloons or dreaming next to dour wives. I wasn't really dour, just blank as an egg, while I sat near the fire burning towards Martha and mending shirts for John. I stopped joining him in bed, but sat up over my sewing until he blew out the lamp.

I had gotten a lock for the sewing chest. I saw John notice it, but he never said a word. I kept pages about Martha under the tray of spools and thimbles and a pile of fabric scraps.

I wrote about her nights after John had gone to sleep. I wrote her hand inside me, I wrote my body arching, I wrote her teeth on my nipples and her hair in my mouth. I told lies and made up stories and gave her special powers. She wrestled buffalo and screamed at eagles. I cupped her, formed her softness. She touched the tops of mountains with her languid double chin. She pressed her breasts against my bones. She lifted herself to find my slick tip with her nipple. She parted river waters so people carrying food in baskets could cross. She sank on me with her full weight, and I breathed shallow under her, caught by her substance and her wonder.

She flew. She spoke with angels. She played Jesus in the Bible. She carved a canyon with her tireless hands. She shook and brought forth waters. She sang whales into the ocean. She ploughed the ground with her knee while she rode a ridge and stroked her hands along the surfaces of grasses in the fields.

I became the earth, her instrument—smoothed and dug and brought forth—but I wrote her powers into her, and played her every night. The mornings were rushed and secret, bordered on all sides with commerce, but at night I made her stretch across me until we filled most open places I could imagine in this world.

I was in the barn churning water to clean the paddle when John came after me. It was not quite dawn. He pushed open the door and kicked the churn away. The paddle snapped off in my hands.

I stood there splattered with milky water, no thought in my head but his name. "John."

He slapped my face hard, then slapped again. I jabbed at his stomach with the splintered end of the paddle. He grabbed my arm and twisted until I dropped it.

"I read your filth," he said, and twisted again.

I was in pain, but there was another feeling. I felt as if I were swelling. I looked down at my arm from a great distance, and saw his hands turning more and more flesh. I felt surrounded by tightness, then heard the fabric of my dress ripping.

I didn't know what was real. My legs were touching. My sleeve hung in tatters. My mouth was open. I was shrieking. I looked at John.

He dropped my arm, breathing hard. His eyes were the usual blue, but strange reds had taken his face.

My face and arm throbbed. I felt my blood wake and beat a motion in every inch of my stretching skin. My breasts were drooping. My sides and back were folding. I was exploding. I was suddenly fat.

John backed away from me, backed into Miss Alice's stall. She looked over her shoulder, her yellow tail switching. He said, "You're a demon."

I understood then that he was terrified, and that I had power in this burst of flesh.

I stepped towards him. "But, John, you are my husband. We must embrace each other." I moved with difficulty, bound wherever my clothes still hung. I felt someone moving with me, someone more graceful in this body, and she used our good arm to loosen the dress collar. It was Martha, but I couldn't tell if she was the living Martha, or the Martha in my stories, or another Martha, who always breathed in me.

John's thick lips were white. He moved them, praying. We reached for him, aware of our dangling upper arms. He shrank back and tripped on the loose hay. He fell. Miss Alice kicked him in the head.

Everything slipped. I was a fat woman watching her attacker drop to the ground, and I was moving inside Miss Alice's muscled back leg, warm under the gold glow that was the surface of light from inside her hide. Then I had a woman's legs again, and tried to run, but I was clumsy and constricted. I fell against a hay bale and looked at the blood seeping through John's white-blond hair.

The waistband of my dress was cutting into me. I saw the folds tighten and constrict. I watched my body shrinking like I was watching water boil—weird, rhythmic motions. My skin pulled in against my bones. The fat slipped to nothing, and with it went the being who had been thinking in my head. I was left with my own large hips and small breasts, my clothes in tatters, my right arm throbbing, and my husband still as ice on the floor.

My legs were their own shape, but they were shaky. I concentrated hard as I walked out the door. I wanted to run, but I could barely make my way across the grass. The wind felt alien on my face, as if I had been inside a churn and now was poured out to sour on the ground.

I made it to the house, cold and in pain. I opened the stove to start a fire, then let it swing half shut. I couldn't stay here, so there was no reason to make it warm. I thought that John could make a fire for himself, then I shivered. Thread and cloth and papers thick with my handwriting were scattered on the floor. The sewing chest stood unlocked. John must have waited for my first careless morning to search for the thing I was keeping to myself.

I went into the bedroom and took off my dress. It was ripped to tatters, but I wasn't sure. Had John ripped it? Had I torn it to pieces in fury? Had I really expanded to three times my size? My arm was swollen and purple. I put on my loosest dress, then used my nightgown to tie my arm to my side in a makeshift splint. Every movement was difficult. I worried John would wake and come after me again. I put on my cloak and went back into the sitting room. There must have been embers beneath the ashes, because the stove was crackling with air from the open door. I picked up a page of my writing and threw it in the fire. It lay there white on the ash, until one corner slowly began to turn brown. I was testing my heart, but I had to pull the paper out of the stove. It wasn't my words that had caused the wreckage, but who John was and what I had done.

I couldn't think about what had seemed to cause me to swell into something I wasn't. Miracle or devil's work, it had saved me.

I gathered the pages and rolled them together, then tied them with a piece of black cord. I pushed them into the pocket of my cloak. I looked around the room. There was nothing else I wanted. I turned my back on these things, and hurried as fast as I could out the door.

I was almost to the road before I remembered the money I had hidden in Miss Alice's stall. I had to go back to the barn.

John was lying where he had been when I left. I had to walk around him to get to the loose plank where I kept the can with the butter money. Miss Alice looked at me, wild-eyed, and blew air through her nose. I put my good hand on her back and thanked her for what she had done.

I kept talking softly to Miss Alice while I lifted the plank to find the can. It was there, and heavy enough to give me hope. I could see John's chest moving, so I knew he was breathing. That fact both relieved and scared me, but I took time to cover the plank with hay again.

Miss Alice bawled when I stood up. I was afraid that John would stir. She turned to follow me out of the barn, stepping delicately over John. I stopped, and she nuzzled my skirt. I had been dreaming over her milk for months as I churned it into love and money. It was crazy to take her with me, but I couldn't leave her for John to wake up to, not after she'd kicked him in the head.

I tied a rope around her neck, and we escaped, almost innocent, from the barn.

On the road, I felt like Miss Alice and I were the Holy Family fleeing to Egypt, without a baby, without a husband, without God. I looked at the weak light, and realized that it was still very early in the morning. Most people would be at their milking or their prayers or still in bed. I hurried to get to Martha's without being seen.

I led Miss Alice around the back into the garden and tied her rope to the fence. I stroked her nose, and she blew warm air on my palm. "Don't eat the kale, Miss Alice. We don't want to wear out our welcome."

Martha's door looked distorted, and kept shrinking as I walked towards it, until I didn't think that I would be able to fit through it at all. "If I can't get in, Martha could never get out," I thought. The door popped back up to scale when I raised my fist to knock.

A fat man with curly grey hair answered the door in his vest. "This is a private entrance," he said. "Service people come in through the store."

His tone was brusque. I stood there, waiting for him to vanish and my mind's tricks to turn kind.

He raised his voice. "Are you deaf?"

I said, "Mrs. Moody, please." I put my hand on the door to keep it from changing shape.

He made a sound in his teeth like the Reverend makes at drunken men he passes on the sidewalk, swatted the door impatiently with his napkin, and called over his shoulder, "Martha, there's a person at the garden door."

I saw her black skirt lapping the stairs before I saw her face. She looked compressed in the hallway behind him, then she moved him gently aside and stepped out to me.

"Why, Amanda, it's not butter day," she said.

Her words almost knocked me over. She looked like living comfort to me, but I couldn't get past her doorstep. I staggered and tried to reach both arms to her, and she noticed that my right one was tied to my side.

"You're hurt," she said. Then finally, a mercy. She took my hand. "Come in."

The man moved aside for her. They were of the same stature, and she could barely squeeze past him. "Excuse me, father," she said. "Mrs. Linger must lie down. She needs our aid." Martha took me upstairs to her bedroom. Her father didn't try to stop her, but he followed at our heels. "There's an animal in the garden," he said as if Miss Alice were repellent and dangerous. "What about that cow?"

With her famous composure, Martha answered, "Perhaps you could find a boy to take the cow to the stables."

I managed to speak. "A doctor. Someone needs a doctor in the barn."

He hooked his thumbs in his vest and gazed at me. I realized I had hay on my skirt and in my hair. My face was hot as well, perhaps where John had slapped me, perhaps where Martha's father's eyes raised my blood.

She helped me to sit on her bed, then looked at him standing on the threshold. "Please, father. Tell the doctor it's the Linger place. And ask him to come by here before he goes."

I leaned back against the headboard. "After."

Martha touched my hair. "All right. After."

Her father snorted, then he left the door.

Martha lifted my legs onto the bed and helped me lie down. She put a pillow under my swollen arm. "He hurt you."

My lashes were sticking together and my face was wet. "Hold me."

So Martha climbed into the snowy sheets in her black dress with her shoes on. I felt for her softness and found enough to let me slip to sleep.

———

I dreamed of straddling Miss Alice on a small saddle with stirrups set to exactly the right length for me. I'm wearing a thick skirt cinched at the waist, leather gloves and a rumpled ten-gallon hat. Miss Alice lifts her head and points her ears like a horse. Then I'm holding onto the saddle horn as Miss Alice swims a river. It is wide and the current is high. I can't see the shore. Miss Alice lurches in the water. I hear her gasping. She's too tired, I think, and let go. The saddle floats away with me, and Miss Alice sinks like a stone until just the ridge of her back is above the surface. I try to reach her again, but the current carries me away toward the falls.

I barely opened my eyes when the doctor bandaged my arm. We didn't speak. I didn't ask about John, although it nagged at my numb brain as the wifely thing to do. I didn't care how John was, but even in my state of collapse I knew that I would have to care soon what other people thought.

I woke again to voices. One of them was Martha's.

"This is my home, Father, and she is welcome here."

"I tell you, it's bad for business. You don't want to be associated with any sort of messiness or immorality."

"She's my friend. Please remember that."

"Why do you insist on lowering yourself? I raised you to associate with the finest people, and here you are in this dusty town, taking up with the wife of some brutish farmer."

His voice rose in round tones as if he was giving an oration. I heard Martha ask for quiet, but she was without her usual authority. I rubbed the fingers of my free hand over the stiff cover of Martha's volume of Shakespeare. The echo of Martha calling me a "friend" thumped in my temples under the bruise. I felt both reduced and detached. I opened the book and saw the bold inscription inside the cover: "To Martha, my Miranda, as she turns thirteen. Father."

Martha had said little about her father. She had told me he had not wanted her to marry her husband, and that he was a businessman back East. Once, when we were lingering in her morning bed while an early customer jangled the handle of the locked front entrance, she had spoken of sliding down a banister smooth as the skin of a cherry, and how her father would catch her at the bottom and laugh. Apart from that, he had not come up. After such silence, it seemed strange that he would travel so far for a visit.

Their words went on, more softly and more tense. I had stopped listening. I couldn't stay in Martha's bed with her father in the house. She had only one spare room. It had to be full of the trunks and other trappings of a pompous man.

I was wearing one of Martha's flannel nightgowns, and it kept slipping over my shoulder and getting caught in the bandage on my arm. I pulled it tight to my neck, wondering where to go and how long the money from the tin can would buy me lodging. If my respectability was in question, then good rooming houses wouldn't take me. My choice would be limited to a few dim rooms over the saloon.

The nightgown surrounded me with the faint smell of Martha's body. I wished she would come upstairs instead of arguing about me with her father. I wanted to look at her awhile.

I pulled the big book into my lap and awkwardly opened it. It fell to a page near the back, and I read:

> *Be not afeard; the isle is full of noises,*
> *Sounds and sweet airs, that give delight and hurt not.*
> *Sometimes a thousand twangling instruments*
> *Will hum about mine ears, and sometime voices*
> *That, if I then had waked after long sleep,*
> *Will make me sleep again; then, in dreaming,*
> *The clouds methought would open and show riches*
> *Ready to drop upon me, that, when I waked*
> *I cried to dream again.*

I hadn't been raised on Shakespeare as I had been on the Bible, but the words stirred me like a strong psalm. Martha had whispered it to me the night I had come to her from the wrecked saloon, but now I shivered under a yearning to be writing miraculous stories next to my stove instead of waiting in Martha's bed.

Martha slept on a cot in the store that night. I heard every movement of her father in the spare room and the hall. In the morning Martha knocked softly, then came in. She shut the door behind her and knelt beside the bed. She was as I knew her—without words—as she rubbed my tears up my cheeks with her open lips. She slid her hand into the loose neck of the nightgown. Her fingers ran light paths across my breasts. I closed my eyes and thought nothing, but I wondered if she were tracing invisible marks that my swelling had left.

"There's someone here to see you," she said. "Do you feel up to it?"

I thought about answering a long time before I could. "Who?"

Martha fluttered her fingers in a tiny imitation. "Clara Spencer."

"Water into wine," I thought. I wanted to see Clara.

I got up and dressed. My arm was tender and awkward, but manageable. I stuck my roll of stories more deeply into my pocket, and went down to meet Clara in the kitchen.

Martha's father stood in the hallway and watched me emerge from her room. I didn't look at his face, but I felt him behind me. I could hear his pocket watch ticking as I stepped carefully down the stairs.

Clara had brought me cream and flowers. "I milked Miss Alice," she said. "I had Clay fetch her when I heard that someone was paying to keep her at the stables."

I squeezed the stems of the columbines in my good hand. "Your kindness continues to surprise me."

Clara got up and started opening cupboards, looking for a vase and sizing up Martha's china. She found an empty jar, and took the flowers from me. "Amanda, I was hurt that you came clear down here to Moody's. If there's anything you need, ask me, you hear?"

I stood up and held onto the back of my chair. "Clara, I can't go back to that house. Could I stay with you and Clay for a while?"

Clara put the jar with flowers and water on the table. When she took my hand, she left droplets on my wrist. "Please come, Amanda. We'd be glad to have you." She hugged me and whispered, "I don't care what you did."

I was ready to leave and had nothing to pack. Clay was waiting with the buggy. Clara went outside to speak with him, and I went into the store to find Martha.

She was selling seed potatoes. I waited until the farmer hauled the sacks away, then I told her I was going to stay with Clara.

Martha said, "I want you here." Her hands were below the counter, and they were moving slightly, as if she were fingering something.

"The Spencers have a spare room that's not occupied." I meant to sound practical, but Martha winced.

"I don't know how long my father will be here," she said. "His business has collapsed."

"John broke the churn." I was sticking to the facts. "I won't be bringing butter."

Martha brought my satin bonnet from beneath the counter. Her hands ran over its surface, as if they couldn't stop. "You left this here. Do you need it?"

I shrugged. "No, I don't need it. Keep it for me, will you?" She bent to put it back on its shelf, and I closed my eyes before the white part in her red hair. I couldn't face another loss that specific.

Martha's father walked up the aisle from the back of the store, then stopped at the glass case empty of butter. I nodded at him. He fingered his vest buttons and watched me as I left.

Six

The sheriff paid me a visit at Clara's. She spotted him coming up the hill, and sent Clay to talk with him. Clara and I watched out the upstairs window while they talked on the porch, then they both kicked the mud off their boots and went into the sitting room.

Clara started circling me, messing with my hair, tucking in my blouse, and smoothing wrinkles out of my skirt. "You didn't do anything," she said. "You've got nothing to worry about."

I stood still for it all with a pounding heart. We had heard nothing about John, although Clay had been to the place, and said it looked as if he had left. I knew that the doctor would have told me if he were dead.

After a short time, Clay called up the stairs. "Amanda, would you come down, please?"

He stood looking up at me with his stubbled face. Clay had received me with kindness, but at that moment I hated his mild expression and his arm reaching towards me to guide me down the last few steps.

Clay led me into the sitting room and directed me to the sofa. I felt childish as I sank into the pattern of flowers and vines, and I let my face settle into a child's lines. My chin trembled whether I let it or not.

The sheriff stood with his own chin in his hands. He was dwarfed by Clay's stuffed chair, so he stayed next to the footstool. He nodded at Clay, who left and shut the door.

"I'm sorry to hear about your troubles, Mrs. Linger."

"Thank you for your concern." It was the first time I could remember looking up at the sheriff. I'd looked directly at him seated at church potluck suppers, but usually his eyes came just below my nostrils. It had made me self-conscious when he used to ask me to dance.

"I've spoken with your husband."

That shook me. "How is John?" Tears came to my eyes. Good, I thought, feel something.

The sheriff looked at his boots. "He regained consciousness last night. He's staying with the Reverend. Could you tell me what happened?"

I felt myself start to tremble, so I took a deep breath and concentrated on the memory of two-stepping with the sheriff as he gazed ardently upwards. I sat as straight as I could in the sofa's embrace, and spoke.

"It was an awful thing. Miss Alice has always been gentle, but John was milking her while I was cleaning the churn, and we could tell that something had spooked her. John actually said something to me about it." My voice caught. John was conscious, and had talked to the sheriff. "Did he tell you that?" The sheriff had stepped to the window and was looking across Clay's fields while he listened to me. "It might be easier if you give me the whole thing before we talk about John."

I heard an undertone of sympathy in his voice. It occurred to me that if John was well, then there was no crime. My voice got stronger. "Miss Alice kicked him. I didn't see it happen, but when I turned I saw him on the hay with blood running from his head."

He was looking at his fingernails. I could see that they were even and smooth. "What did you do?"

"I ran to John, but I couldn't wake him. I went to town to fetch the doctor. I thought that would be the quickest thing. I took Miss Alice so she couldn't hurt him again. I wasn't thinking clearly."

The sheriff came closer. He stood over me. "Why did you go to Moody's?"

I wasn't thinking, just lying. "It was the first place I saw people stirring. It was very early."

He scratched his neck. "What happened to your arm? The doctor tells me it's broken."

My arm. I had forgotten it, although it was throbbing in a sling across my chest. "Miss Alice was still excited when I went to help John. She stepped on my arm."

The sheriff took a couple of steps away from me. He examined his hands again. "Mrs. Linger, you're not a woman used to lying. I can see that." I bit my lip. He continued. "The doctor examined you. That arm is so bruised it looks burned. We found a broken churn handle, which you haven't mentioned. And we found a dress at the house ripped to shreds. Undergarments and all."

He crossed his arms. "Affairs between a man and his wife are their business. But nobody's going to think less of you if you stay away from John Linger." He made a noise between his teeth. "The man doesn't even drink."

My face was hot, and I kept my eyes to my lap. I felt shame that people knew that John didn't cherish me, that he had treated me rough. "What does John say?" He must have told them that I had written stories about the taste of another woman's breasts.

The sheriff rubbed his chin. "I don't think he really remembers what happened. He's not right in the head. He gets hysterical at any mention of you. He claims you turned into a monster. There's talk of women wrestling buffalo and dancing on clouds. He doesn't want to see you because he thinks you're the devil himself."

Clara was writhing with questions, but I didn't speak about John. She let me be. We didn't talk of anything more difficult than whether to fix cabbage-and-sausage or salt pork for supper. Clara was endlessly curious, even about the sex lives of chickens and yard cats, but she didn't pry at me. I was grateful. She was protecting me at the expense of her ruling vice, and I helped her at her chores with love and relief.

I didn't leave Clara's land. People kept their distance. The sheriff had been gentle, but he talked over whiskey the way Clara talked over tea, and I knew the story must have gotten out. I didn't care that John thought I was the devil, but I wanted to know what I thought myself before I faced the people of Moody. I knew that there were plenty who held that a woman should cleave unto her husband no matter what he did. I considered this one night as I sat on the edge of the bed in Clara's back room, surprised to find how little of it I believed. I had borrowed the Bible from the front parlor, and now I opened it to Genesis, trying to get to the root of things, to find the old story about how woman came to be, and how much she might owe man because of it, but instead I stopped on Noah, on how the sons of God came into the daughters of man, who bore them children. That, along with giants in the earth, was the main reason given for God's feeling that He needed a flood.

It didn't sit right with me, although it should have seemed a small thing: that the sons were of God and the daughters were of man nagged me with its inaccuracy. I read a little further, daubing my fingers in warm wax from the candle, until I found a verse whose moment I recognized:

In the six hundreth year of Noah's life, in the second month, the seventeenth day of the month, the same day were all the fountains of the great deep broken up, and the windows of heaven were opened.

This had happened to me. I had been drenched by the fountains of the great deep, in this middle part of my life after I had known what things were supposed to be like for me, sometime before my six hundreth year. I wasn't sure if it had happened when I carried my best butter to Martha in a flowered bowl, or when she had splashed soapy water up the insides of my legs, or when I had written about an angel with the yellow body of a cow, or when I had walked with Miss Alice away from the barn, but I had spilled some mystery that had made my life change.

I wrote about Martha. I couldn't stop. I kept the stories John had seen rolled up beneath the mattress. I never looked back through them. I wrote a new one every night. I knew from Clara that Martha's father was working in the store, standing next to the cash register more than Martha did herself. I wondered whether she had moved my bonnet from its shelf beneath the counter, or if he were free to nuzzle it with his fingers between sales.

In one story Martha breathed on a green tree and burned all of its leaves to ash.

Miss Alice was in the pasture with Clay's horses and mule. She was off her feed, upset with the changes. Maybe she missed John. I spent as much time with her as I could, lingering over the little splatter of milk she gave me, stroking her with my hand since I hadn't thought to bring her comb.

One morning I came down to the barn and found her hay threaded with black-eyed Susans. She was chewing on one with her old calm rhythm. I hadn't seen the flowers when I had brought her water the night before.

Another morning I was out in the yard gathering eggs when I saw Martha climbing the hill to the house. She walked slowly, her black skirt rippling with the grasses.

I put the warm egg I held back into the nest, and went down to meet her. She took my hand.

"You look well, Amanda. Has your arm healed?" She was subdued, wearing a fringed scarf that covered her hair.

"It's still tender, but the doctor removed the bandages a week ago." I kept my eyes on the low grasses. She moved her thumb lightly back and forth across my wrist, and it was as if she were brushing my whole body with light.

She looked at my face, and even that felt like a touch. "I've missed you."

I tightened as my pride hit me. "Why did you stay away, then?"

Martha let go of my hand. "I didn't know if you'd want me here. I was ashamed that I hadn't asked you to stay with me."

I looked towards the house and saw Clara at the window. "Will you come inside?"

Martha shook her head. "I have an offer to make you, but first I need to tell you how things are between me and my father. I couldn't do that with Clara over tea."

So we sat down on the grass in front of the house and its windows while Martha told me how her father had shaped her life.

He had been a self-made man, and she was his ticket upwards in the social world, but even as a girl, she was willing to be only her own ticket. He had loved her with cold pride, and she had taken luxury for granted. She had passed easily through the great house that was her birthright. He watched her slide her hand along the walnut stair rail that the servants polished to velvet. He could see that the softness didn't startle her—she expected it from anything her hands used.

Her mother had died when she was six. Her absence was quiet in their lives, but Martha felt it. She had her mother's hair and her father's jaw.

Practically from birth, she had played with the watch that hung from his silk waistcoat, and listened to his rich voice surround words with importance. But even as a toddler sitting in his lap, holding the ticking watch, she had felt resentment. As she got older, it became more acute. She felt the weight of his plans and his persistent hand in her life. Martha's father was silent about what he wanted from her, but she was to marry wealth. That much was as clear as consommé, and she had sucked it from her spoon since she was her mother's butterball.

He let her go on errands alone as a young woman, perhaps, said Martha, out of fear that he had raised her too softly. She could not know how harshly she would be judged as a wife and mother if she moved, as he wanted her to, among the great families, in the heart of old money and old power. To toughen her up, he let Martha out on the streets alone; he thought that at worst she might be robbed.

What happened was, for him, almost worse than violence. Martha bought some fabric in a dry goods store and found Wilbur Moody, full of spit and vinegar and ardor for the West. Her father forbade them to marry, then relented to prevent elopement, but he gave them a diminished wedding that Martha knew was an insult, because she was marrying a shopkeeper. A maiden lady had played the organ, and that was all. Martha had worn blue. Wilbur had trotted through his paces in a white shirt with thin pink stripes, oblivious to the nuances, until Martha was left in bed with a man whom she respected only when in motion. A few weeks later, they packed up a wagon and went.

Before they left, her father gathered men in tailcoats and women in satin slippers to hear his daughter's final recitation. Perhaps he was aching for the days when her promise had been so clear. Wilbur wandered away from the revellers to sit among the marigolds in the garden. Though he was used to feeling prosperous, he was diminished in the great hall with the feathers and champagne. He thought about what he'd read of California and felt the hard pull across the plain. His foot itched. He couldn't wait to go west.

Inside, Martha made her entrance under the molded ceiling. Her cheeks were ruddy, and her white lace gown drifted from her hips to the floor. Her father, enthroned in a big walnut chair, clapped his hands for silence. The faces around him shone like new nickels.

She lifted her chin, so like his, and gazed at the ceiling as if it were her text. The room grew hushed. Suddenly she lowered her head and faced the audience. *"The Tempest,"* she announced.

She sent Ariel's song to her father in a whispery voice that had ladies covering their mouths with their fans.

> *Full fathom five thy father lies;*
> > *Of his bones are coral made;*
> *Those are pearls that were his eyes:*
> > *Nothing of him that doth fade*
> *But doth suffer a sea-change*
> *Into something rich and strange.*
> *Sea-nymphs hourly ring his knell:*
> > > *Ding-dong.*
> *Hark, now I hear them——Ding-dong, bell.*

By the time she finished, she had practically crawled into his lap. She stood in front of him looking at her feet during the applause, then raised her hand for silence. When it came, she pointed at his watch, or heart, and screeched into his face:

> *Why, as I told thee, 'tis a custom with him*
> *I'th' afternoon to sleep. There thou mayst brain him,*
> *Having first seiz'd his books, or with a log*
> *Batter his skull, or paunch him with a stake,*
> *Or cut his wezand with thy knife.*

Her father rose, smiling blandly, and began to clap. It was not clear that she had finished, but the others joined in. Young Miss Jenner, with whom her father had been flirting, gave Martha a lily and complimented her on her delivery. He himself said nothing, but she knew by his silence that he suffered from her performance. Wilbur ambled in from the garden after it was over, and quickly joined the applause.

Martha had many long hours of travel, and later, of work, in which to consider her behavior and that of her father. She concluded that she had been spoiled and petulant. Over the years while alone, building her business and losing her taste for theatrics, she had written him her first letters, telling him of her success, and asking for news of home.

He had answered after some months, in a letter short on news and long on dignity, but eventually they established a stately correspondence. When his business failed, Martha had known that he would come to Moody.

I was overwhelmed by Martha's sudden flood of words. I could picture her as an orator—she always had presence—but I couldn't imagine her under the thumb of a patriarch. "Martha," I said, "you're a full-grown woman."

"You should know," she said, and we both laughed. In broad daylight under Clara's bedroom window, she put her arms around me, and I leaned back against her.

"He's very difficult," she said, stroking my hair, "but his whole world has collapsed. I owe him the comfort I can give him. He protected me when I was young."

I became conscious of movement behind us, and turned to see the curtains fluttering. I couldn't see Clara's face, but I sat up, out of Martha's arms.

Martha thought I had understood something. "So that's why I can't see you in the way we were before, even though I long to, especially after all you've suffered at the hands of your husband."

I put my arms around my knees and looked down the hill. "Why did you come up here, to tell me that? I knew I hadn't seen you. I didn't need the story of your girlhood. I didn't need you holding my damned hand."

Martha stood up. "I saw you, and I wanted to touch you. I came up here for a reason."

I got to my feet, too. "Well, you've finished, so why don't you go."

She pushed the fringe out of her eyes and put her hands on her hips. I watched her gather herself into Martha Moody, Proprietress. "I came to offer you a job," she said.

"What?" I was stunned.

Her tone was formal. "I don't know if you have any money. You could work at the store, if you want to."

I sent her away, but in the morning asked Clay to take a note to the store accepting her offer.

Clara couldn't believe it. "Amanda, what possessed you to take a job in the public eye? It's much too soon after the separation for you to appear ringing up soap and tobacco."

I took a few stitches on the overskirt of the dress we were making for her. "Clara, I don't have much money. You and Clay can't afford to feed me for nothing. The old farm belongs to John, and I couldn't work it if it were mine. What else can I do?"

I thought I sounded confident, like a practical woman with sound reasons for her actions. Clara couldn't know that I was defying every rule of logic and nature, but she looked at me as if she did know, as if she were harboring a lunatic.

She dabbed at her nose with a lace handkerchief. "You're not meant for commerce, Amanda. You're meant for higher things."

I jabbed my finger with the needle. "Obviously not a wife's sacred duties." I pulled a scrap of flannel from the sewing chest to stop the blood.

Clara leaned over to me with earnest intensity. Above her high collar, her face was concerned. "You can flout convention," she said, "but only if you're answering to a more powerful master."

I sucked my finger. "I have no idea what you're talking about, Clara. What do you mean?"

Clara sewed with thimbles on both hands, and now she clinked them against each other. "Love," she said. "Art. God. In the service of these, you must do what they dictate, within the bounds of conscience, even if it takes you outside the society of good people."

Clara's face was flushed and excited. I put my hand on her arm to stop her thimbles from tinkling. "Don't get overwrought. Isn't this a rather elevated reaction to a position dusting shelves at the general store?"

Clara stuck her legs out and crossed them at the ankles. "Well, I'll miss you while you're polishing milk bottles at Martha Moody's all day long, but if it's something you have to do, I won't complain."

I stuck my needle in the cushion, took the fabric from her lap, and succumbed to an urge to put an end to Clara's philosophical flights by tickling her. Clay was roused from his back-porch cigar by shrieks, and came to find us in a wriggling pile on the rug, laughing.

That night I wrote a story about young Martha with her father in another world:

> When Martha was a young woman, before she knew the extent of her powers, she wore trousers and swaggered on the dark, wooded lands of her father's estate. She carried her bow and arrow, but she was not a silent walker. She tromped and whistled at the birds to scare them. She scattered buckets of sunflower seed in a clearing, so that when she burst into it, she would raise a crowd of wings.
>
> Her father sometimes followed her with his soft steps, standing back in the shadows. He would time her progress with his gold watch, waiting for her to arrive at the river. He always gave up while she was still tromping through the woods, but he knew she went there, because he had looked out his window and seen the water change color. He had seen her footprints on the bank.
>
> Martha talked to the river. Her father didn't find her because she swam for many miles. When she got tired, she took off her trousers, tied the legs, and blew them up for floats. Then she rested on them and went farther down the river. Her breasts bobbed beneath her linen shirt.
>
> She told the river all her problems: how her father watched her, how she felt like a plump fruit. She told it how she cried with

frustration because after she hit a target in archery, she had to blush and apologize if anyone had seen. She said she made noises in the woods because when animals fled she knew that she had been there.

Sometimes she churned the water, kicking the bottom with her heels. She raised red mud, and her father at his window saw a change in the color of the river.

The river was patient, but confused about mercy. Emotions floated in a green film on its surface. They felt much like water bugs: skittery things, hard to ignore when it passed under them.

It decided to help her. Almost always a mistake, from a river. It caught Martha floating on her back and washed over her. It splashed her face and poured into her mouth. Martha had been saying she hated her fat waist, but now she struggled and sputtered. She beat her arms and got her head in the air, but the river tangled her foot in the root of a willow, so she was trapped while her face was washed in walls of water. Finally it subsided, leaving Martha limp against the mud and willow roots. She got her foot out and struggled up the bank. Then she stretched out exhausted on the grass and slept.

When she woke, she walked the miles home, silent and bedraggled. Her father said nothing when he saw her straggle in. Martha still loved the water. She loved to feel it lap her, but now when she spoke she felt the waves washing all breath from her mouth. That is how Martha lost her voice, why she speaks only when she has to. She swallowed so much water that it mixed with her blood, and that's where she gets her motion and her power to encompass and her endless force like a river washing against its bank.

Seven

The brass bells jangled when I walked into the store, looking as respectable as possible in my fresh-washed dress, the one I had fled in. Martha's father reached under the counter and handed me an apron. "Mrs. Linger, isn't it? Put this on."

The apron was so stiff with starch that I had a hard time tying the strings. Martha's father came around the counter, his watch chain shimmering, his big hands waving over the half-empty barrel of dried beans. "Start by refilling the barrels."

The store cat, Bathsheba, was curled up in the tea crate. The complex coffee-lavender-kerosene smell of the place was the same as it had been every morning that Martha had accepted my butter and taken me up to her room. I took a deep breath, and said, "I don't believe we've been formally introduced."

He hooked his fingers in the pockets of his vest, and said, "Oh yes. I'm Charles Balm. Mr. Balm. The last time we saw each other, you were in too much distress for introductions." I must have flinched, because he added, "Your arm has recovered, I trust?"

I ignored his question. "Martha is expecting me. May I ask where she is?"

He rested one hand on the rim of the bean barrel. "She's busy in her office with her accounts. I'll be overseeing your duties."

I wanted to throw his apron on the floor and rattle the bells on my way out, but Martha, who was behind the door to the back office, had asked me to come. She stuck her head out and said hello as her father led me to the cellar where the sacks of grains were kept. I turned to answer, but she had already shut the door.

So I bent over the barrels, tipping them on their sides to get the dregs into a sack so I could dump them onto the top of each barrel again when I had filled it up. Beans, oats, crackers, raisins, chewing tobacco. Mr. Balm stood next to the cash register taking care of customers and watching me work. I didn't look up when the brass bells rang, and no one spoke to me. I wiped sugar from my hands onto my apron, then split open a sack of flour. I leaned into the thought that I was working for Martha. A few months ago, this would have been joy past anything I could have imagined. I tried to pretend that I was building soft mountains of love as I poured the flour into the barrel, but I wasn't settled in enough to dream.

I smoothed off the top of the flour. Bathsheba the cat darted into the sack at my feet, and came out with a mouse struggling between her teeth.

Martha's father put his hand on my shoulder. "You need to sweep."

I took the broom and moved away from him. The cat slipped past my skirts.

He watched me. "Don't dawdle." His lips seemed a half beat slower than his words. I wondered how he liked minding the counter like a common clerk. Martha had always seemed serene and distant, handing out change as if from a mountaintop. Her father looked fussy. I saw children peer in the window at his long-jowled face and decide not to stop.

I swept up grains and dust around the barrels. I felt Mr. Balm's eyes on me as I worked the floor in front of the candy bins: striped sticks, rock candy, sugar almonds, gum drops. He said, "Mrs. Linger, you missed the corner," and I pushed faster towards the back of the store.

I could see Martha's outline through the yellow glass panel in her office door. She was in silhouette, bent over her desk as if deep in concentration. I scratched at the base of the door with the broom, but she didn't look up.

I lingered there as long as I could, straightening the magazines and dusting off pill bottles: Pierce's Little Pellets; Easy Things to Take; Ward Off Bilious Fevers; and the Ague Shakes.

I moved on to yard goods, where Martha's father couldn't see me because of the tall bolts of cloth. The yard goods picked up the smells of kerosene, cinnamon, salt pork, red pepper and coffee. At home, I always sniffed the fabric and thought of Martha before I cut out a pattern. I kept sweeping, past the fancy lamp with the decorated base and the candles and the flypaper. Bathsheba was curled up in the onion bin, finished with her mouse. I bent over to herd onion skins into the dustpan, then heard a footstep in the aisle behind me and felt Martha's father press himself against me.

I stood up, biting back a yell. We were out of sight of Martha's door. He pushed me against the shelf, grabbing at my breasts. Bathsheba stood up on the onions, and I heard the brass bells tinkle just as I picked up the cat and threw her into Mr. Balm's face. She went claws first, lashing at his cheek. "Great God Almighty!" Mr. Balm shouted.

I shoved past him towards the back of the store. The cat had disappeared. I looked back and saw Theda Wilks rushing to where Martha's father stood with his hand to his face. Martha opened her office door, and stared as I took the narrow hall through the kitchen and out the door that opened onto the garden with the alley behind.

I went down to the creek before I climbed the hill to Clara's house. I wasn't ready to speak. My skin was burning, so I knelt and dipped both hands into the water. The cold kicked across my wrists, and I took a deep breath. I reached all of the way to the bottom and dug my fingers into the thick silt. I leaned there crying with my hands buried and my knees damp until the shame cooled off.

When I finally pulled my hands from the mud and rinsed them in the water, I heard a rustling behind me. I turned and looked behind me at the thick roots of a willow that cut into the overhanging bank. There was a large hole between the roots, and I saw eyes glinting at me from inside. Our gaze held for a moment, then whatever it was scrambled further back into the den. I left the creek with my arms half-rinsed.

I got to Clara's with wet sleeves and muddy stains on the apron. I came in the front door and slipped upstairs, hoping that Clara wouldn't hear me from the kitchen, but we startled each other in the hall outside the spare room where I had been sleeping.

Clara put her hand to her mouth when she saw me. "Amanda, what are you doing home so soon?" Her eyes slid over my stained clothing. "What happened?"

I wanted to go into my room to change, but Clara took my arm and pulled me away to the kitchen. I let her lead me to a chair. Clara was half my size, but she lowered her shoulder and pushed me in the direction she wanted me to go, and I always went.

She took the muddy apron off me and threw it into the wash basket. "What happened?" she asked again.

I looked into her avid face. "I found the working conditions unacceptable."

Clara shook her head and thrummed her small fingers against the table. "Did Martha ask you to pour sand in the sugar?"

"Martha's father was disrespectful." My arms were leaving damp spots on Clara's tablecloth. "He is a lecher."

Clara raised an eyebrow, but she didn't look surprised. "She'll lose trade if she keeps letting him take a hand in the store. This is a decent community."

I took her hand. "Clara, I must ask you not to repeat this story. My honor is compromised enough, and I don't want Martha's business to suffer."

"I swear I won't speak of it." Clara gave my hand a squeeze. "But he looks so ominous behind the counter." She sounded slightly thrilled, as if she'd just read a garish story in one of her ladies' magazines.

I saw the excitement in her face, but I also saw genuine kindness. "I don't know what I'll do for money, Clara, but I'll think of something."

She let go of my hand and gave me a mysterious look. "Don't worry too much about it. Something will come up."

I flicked my fingers at her across the table. "What are you plotting, Clara? Sending me and Miss Alice to join the circus as an animal act?"

She wiped her hands on her apron. "You don't have to imagine outlandish adventures, Amanda. You have plenty in real life." She laughed nervously. I looked at her small face and wondered if Clara had adventures of her own.

That night I sat in my nightgown in the spare room and read about Jezebel being thrown to the dogs as Clay and Clara rustled about touching furniture and speaking softly to each other before they went to sleep. Then I wrote:

One day Martha Moody was walking in the creek, listening to its quiet sounds. She was wearing her black skirt and shawl, and she was thinking about her business. The water painted women with fishtails all around her ankles, but Martha didn't notice. She was reliving the moment when she had finished her accounts, and the figures had looked so elegant appearing in black ink beneath her fingers. She rounded down the total in her head, to be safe.

Her father floated just under the surface of the creek as a wide shadow. He was diaphanous, and could have been the reflection of a cloud, except for his gold watch chain, which trailed along the creek bed, stirring the loose mud. Martha held her skirts closer to her legs. She felt as though she were about to catch on a branch, but she didn't slow her steps. She added the key figures in her head again: first quarter sales, groceries; first quarter sales, dry goods.

Rain began to dimple the creek. Martha's father blurred and broke down into the shadows of water striders that sped away from each other. Martha looked at the sky.

He was there again, stretched above her like a rainbow across the flat white of the storm clouds. His colors began to shimmer when she saw him——the green-and-bronze check of his vest, the soft gold of his chain, the rich brown cloth of his suit.

Martha climbed out of the water and stood under a tree. The limbs made patterned lines across her father and the sky. The rain dampened her blouse. Her father's face was red and cumulous. He looked at her, and the wind blew gaps in his eyes. He reached his hand towards the earth, towards her.

Martha wrapped her arms around the tree and held tight. She wished that she could turn into a mushroom clinging to the bark, but Martha's powers let her take only her true form. His filmy hand made its slow way from the heights. Martha found a foothold, and began to climb the tree.

She had reached a strong lower limb when she heard thuds and slow movement along the creek bank. Her cloud father looked toward the sounds, and his hand stopped. A large cow with yellow wings and a yellow tail was walking placidly along the bank. The cow had a long tongue with which she licked her nose, and yellow-gold eyes that seemed to be watching reflections in the water.

"Azreal!" shouted Martha from her branch.

The cow didn't look up. She just kept plodding along, grazing on moss, leaving hoofprints in the mud. Martha tossed twigs at her back to get her attention, but Azreal just flicked her tail, oblivious.

Martha's father grabbed the top of her tree, and pulled himself level with her. He bounced in the subsiding breeze like a balloon on a tether. His waistcoat was pierced by branches at several places, but Martha felt him settling all around her like a cold fog. She could hear his watch ticking.

Azreal passed under the tree. Martha crouched on her limb, thinking to jump onto the cow's back, but Azreal suddenly folded her legs beneath her and sat down on the edge of the bank, chewing her cud.

By now, Martha was deep in her father's cloud, and could barely see the cow's hide shining below on the bank. When she looked at her own hands, they were shaking and mottled with green-and-bronze checks. She began slapping at the air, at the tree, at her own skin, panicked. Her foot slipped. As she lost her balance, she grabbed at the gold chain that was sliding down the bark like a snake. It was cold and solid in her hand, and whipped her out over the creek, then back towards the tree, where she pushed off with her feet to keep from being smashed against the trunk. She hung with her skirts tangled in the links, then caught a limb with her legs and jerked against the chain with her full weight.

A small gold disk tumbled through the air, flipping and spinning as it fell, until it splashed into the water. It was her father's watch, which dug itself into the creek bed and vanished. The chain slipped out of her hands and slithered after it. The air warmed and cleared, and Martha dropped from the limb to the soft bank. Nothing in the water or sky suggested her father.

Azreal looked over her shoulder at Martha. "Powerful stuff," she murmured, then she put her chin back down on the ground.

Martha pushed her hair out of her eyes. In spite of the new sunshine, the creek had formed a sheet of ice, with sudden pockets of air moving beneath it. Martha drew her shawl up around her head, then sat against the cow's warm back to keep watch over the edge of the creek.

Miss Alice was dry one morning, so I brushed the flies off her flank, scratched her forehead, then walked back up the hill to the house. A cold rain had started, so I drew my shawl up over my head and hurried up the back stairs to change my wet shoes before I went to help Clara. I thought she was working in the kitchen because the scent of sugar and baking apples filled the house.

But when I opened the door to the spare room, Clara was kneeling beside my bed. She looked over her shoulder at me, then shoved her hands in her apron pocket, but not before I saw my stories pulled from their hiding place and spread across the floor. There was a smear of wet cinnamon on the last page I had written the night before.

Clara jumped up and stepped towards me. She touched my face and said, "I'm sorry, Amanda."

I brushed the trail of sugar off my cheek, then grabbed her arm. Her grey muslin had a dusting of flour on the sleeve. "What are you doing? What do you think you've done?"

She pulled her arm free and nervously licked a finger. "I've read your stories. I've been reading them for months."

I sat down on the bed, shaking. "You had no right."

Clara reached into her pocket and brought out a writing pad. Her face was red. She tossed the writing pad down on the quilt next to me. "Here."

I picked it up and flipped through it. I knew Clara's handwriting from years of notes and recipes, and caught glimpses of phrases. "A small gold disk . . . she wore trousers . . . her black dress melted away . . . dry rot."

And the name Martha, over and over.

Clara was talking. "I found them one day when I turned your mattress. I wasn't in here looking for anything. At first I was shocked, but I copied them and sent some away to magazines back east. The editor of one of them, *True Western Tales,* wants to publish them."

I looked at Clara leaning against the door frame, keeping her distance and talking a blue streak. "I did it for you," she said. "The adventures are good and you need the money." She wiped her hands on her apron and said, "I edited out the indiscreet parts. It's not a salacious publication."

I punched the mattress. Clara flinched. The quilt was a pattern of stars and diamonds she had tacked down with her even stitch. Looking at it made me sick. I bent over and groped under the bed for my stories and my half-empty money can, grabbed my cloak and stood up to face Clara at the door.

She was crying, and fingering the satin buttons on her cuffs. "Don't go, Amanda. I was going to tell you. I'm still your friend."

Her fingers circling the buttons made me remember Martha's hands touching my nipples. At that moment, it was a horrible thought. "You're a betrayer and a thief," I said, then pushed past her and ran down the stairs.

Clara screamed after me. "I know you. I've read the stories. Has Martha read even one?"

The rain had stopped. I fetched Miss Alice from the barn, and we went home.

Eight

I had been gone for a few months, but it felt like years. I led
Miss Alice to the pasture, but I didn't have to urge her into
the gate. She walked through the high grass to the salt lick and
followed its hollows with her tongue. I filled the water trough
for her. The barn door was standing open, so I was sure that
raccoons and rats and others with appetites had been helping
themselves to the grain. I left it ajar so that Miss Alice could
find her way to her stall. I didn't go into the barn myself.

I was afraid I might find John there, waving his fist. Worse,
I might beg him please not to hurt me. I might find my mouth
open and "sorry" spilling out as if there were no link at all
between what my heart thought and what my body said.

I didn't really expect to see John in the barn, but still I
hurried to the house.

Inside, it smelled like a winter's fires were smoldering in
the walls. The last of the stove wood was gone. My sewing chest
was in its place on the little table with the Bible, still unlatched.

I walked into the bedroom and saw John's clothes next to
mine in the wardrobe. I didn't know where he was. And I didn't
want to know. Clay had come down and fetched some of my
clothes, but most of them were hanging there where they had
been the day I left.

I put on my old red serge, went back into the front room, and sat down in my chair by the stove. I felt a sudden calm, as if the chair and the stove and the sewing chest could protect me, as if they had been protecting me all my married life. I thought again of John in the barn, of Clara reaching for stories under my mattress, of Martha leaning over her books while her father pressed up against me. I wanted protection, and to protect. Then I heard it coming over the garden: a song played softly on a horn.

I went to the door. It was late afternoon. Miss Alice was still grazing quietly in the pasture. The music came to me, in fits and starts with the wind, from the barn.

I ran outside, towards the road. I felt frightened and dizzy, like a child's hoop spinning over and over across the ground. Miss Alice rushed the fence, as if she expected me to take her along. When I ignored her, she opened her mouth and bawled. The music stopped.

I stopped, too. I had no place to go. Miss Alice bawled again. I walked slowly back past the dry garden to the pasture, and opened the gate.

Miss Alice came over to me, and I patted her flank. I pulled a handful of grass and gave it to her. She chewed it a while. I put my arm around her sun-warmed neck and walked with her to the door of the barn.

It was hard to see looking in from the light, but as my eyes adjusted, I made out the outline of the stalls. Miss Alice left me to stand in hers. There was no one in sight, but the stool that John used as a music stand was in the middle of the barn, and the ladder was propped next to the loft.

I didn't know if John had climbed the ladder and was

listening above me, or if he had left over the back fence, but I went full into the barn.

"John, can you hear me?" I heard a rustling like rats in the loft. I used to be frightened of rats, but I had never let them keep me from milking. I saw my churn laying on its side, the broken handle protruding from the lid. Miss Alice was chewing the wood of her stall.

"Stop it, Miss Alice, that's a bad habit." I walked over to the churn and set it upright. "John, this is your wife, Amanda. I've come back to the place, but not to you, and I don't want to see you around here." I listened. The rustling was sharp and constant, but I heard nothing else. "I'll speak to the sheriff if I have to."

Miss Alice looked over her shoulder at me. I knew she was waiting. I took the stool and found the bucket, and sat down by her side to milk her. I kept talking.

"I don't know if you're in here, John, but if you are, I hope you're listening. Go back to the Reverend's, and you'll be fine. You can tell anyone who asks that I'm more addled than you are. Anyone who wants me out of here is going to have to stare down a crazy woman with an axe."

I was talking big, but in the back of my mind, I was thinking that Mrs. Carry A. Nation may have gotten famous swinging a hatchet, but I might just get hurt. I kept milking. I didn't have anything else to say, so I left the barn with a full bucket of milk and held my back straight as I walked to the house. All I heard behind me was rustling.

———

I heard music again as the weeks wore on, but John never showed his face. It was always in bald daylight, so it didn't scare me like it might have at night. I got used to it. He played softly, not the martial hymns from the old days with the band, but tunes I didn't recognize. He didn't come to the barn anymore, but kept to the far corners of the fields. Once I saw him from a distance, his white hair bright as a chip of mica, standing next to a big red rock, facing away from the house, playing.

I didn't like it, but he never got close to me, so I didn't go for the sheriff. I told myself that he just came out here to practice without disturbing the Reverend. I was bound and determined not to waste one more minute of my life messing with him, so I sewed myself a pocket to carry a kitchen knife on the underside of my skirt, and let him be.

I gathered brush for kindling and tried to revive the garden. I talked to Miss Alice every morning and evening, and walked out to the pasture several times a day. I would brush away the flies for her, and go over her hide with her comb.

Miss Alice stayed solid as my world shifted. She was a little less vocal than she used to be, and she moved a little less: standing in the shade of the barn and chewing her cud all day or lying down in the long grass near the water trough, but she always came when I rattled the gate. Maybe she missed John. I liked talking to Miss Alice in the sun, but it wasn't enough.

I spent a lot of time writing stories. I sat in the chair by the stove in broad daylight, and invented lives for Martha. She was heroic. She wrestled wolves. She ran to a prairie fire and put it out with her sweat. She built a house of hollowed pumpkins and kept candles burning inside them all night long.

I became so involved in my inner life that things fell away around me. Martha broke the tips off mountains to use as drinking cups, and my own manners strayed from the etiquette I had learned from Mrs. Luz. Most days I didn't feel like messing with flowered plates, so I ate my meals from the skillet, or from dusty jars.

I was down to a few jars of tomatoes and pickled cucumbers. The only potatoes left were soft and shriveled, trailing long, rooted eyes. I had milk and butter from Miss Alice, but mice had chewed into the flour sack. I couldn't face going to the store, and my money was low. Martha swallowed a summer's worth of grasshoppers, and they jumped in her laugh.

I had started wearing John's coat around the place, the one he had ripped outside the saloon the day Carry Nation came to town. I slipped it on one evening when I went out to milk, and it was warm over my dress. I washed it and mended the ripped sleeve. It had deep pockets and smelled sweet. I was as comfortable in it as I was in the marriage bed without John.

Sometimes I wore his shirts, too. They gave me more room to move than my calicos, and more time before I had to heat up a kettle of water for the wash. I tried on his pants, but they wouldn't fit over my hips, so I kept to skirts. Martha wore the river at her waist as a sash.

The clothes reminded me of John when they were hanging in our wardrobe, but not when I wore them. I had starched and ironed them so many times that they seemed to be more a part of me than him. I left off the starch now, and let the cotton fall in wrinkles around me, with the collar unbuttoned and the tails left untucked more often than not. I was forgetting the look of things for the feel of them, and that is a dangerous thing in this world.

I was sitting in a wooden chair in the doorway, reading the Bible and eating my last jar of tomatoes in the afternoon light, when I saw a girl tearing across the fields towards my house. She ran fast, and her skirt rode her skinny knees above the high grasses. At first I thought she was running for the pleasure of it, but when she cut across my pasture, I knew she was after me.

I had an impulse to duck into the house and put on a blouse and sit at the table like a decent woman, but I just stood up and tucked in the tail of John's white shirt, then sat down again. When she came into the yard, she slowed to a walk, and I closed the book.

She reached into a sleeve of her dress, pulled out an envelope and handed it to me. "Mrs. Spencer sent me to give this to you."

It was damp from the girl's sweat, and had my name on the outside in Clara's neat handwriting. She had stuck "Mrs." on the front of it, to be polite. Looking at it must have wrenched my face. The girl turned to go.

I put a hand on her skinny shoulder. "Wait. Can you read?"

She shook off my hand and backed away from me, glancing at the envelope. "I didn't read anything. It's all sealed up."

"That's not what I mean." I slipped the letter into the Bible, and beckoned her into the house. "Come in for a minute."

She pushed her wild hair out of her face, and said, "Why?"

I walked into the kitchen and poured two glasses of milk, but she stood in the yard scuffing her foot, waiting for an explanation before she did anything else.

I was lonely for company, but I wasn't so far gone to think I could get this child to sit and talk with me, much as I would have liked some conversation. I got some money from the tin can and brought the milk and a scrap of paper back outside.

"My name's Ruth," she said when I handed her the milk. She drank it in fast swallows. "Your cow must be a good milker."

"Potatoes," I wrote, my stomach knotting, "sugar, flour, coffee." I looked at Ruth, who had white on her mouth. "That's Miss Alice. I think I know your mother from church."

"Probably." Ruth licked her lip and looked out over the pasture.

"Molasses. Oats. Dried beans. Matches." I read the list out loud. "Will you buy these things at the store for me? You can keep a nickel for stick candy."

"Yes, ma'am." She took the list and stuffed it in her sleeve.

"Give another nickel to a boy to help you carry everything." I handed her the money. "And don't tell anyone else who these groceries are for."

She fiddled with the coins. "I won't."

"And don't dawdle!" I yelled after her, but she was already halfway to the road. I watched her break into that clean run and wished I were her, a scrawny girl on an errand of no concern to me, moving fast.

I sat back down and picked up the Bible. I opened the envelope, and another envelope fell out, addressed to Clara in a strange hand. She had enclosed a note and a pressed violet. I was mad before I even broke the sealing wax, and that violet made it worse. I missed Clara, but if she thought we could make up over sweet notes and pressed flowers, she was dead wrong. I thought of her face gleaming as she and Theda Wilks crashed the big shelf of liquor bottles to the ground. Clara wasn't as dainty as she made out to be.

I read her note.

> *Amanda,*
> *I didn't open this. I think of you, and hope you are safe and well.*
> *I miss your companionship. You have a gift, and I only thought*
> *to serve it.*
> *With Affection,*
> *Clara*

She sounded so exaggerated and stiff. I crumpled the note and picked up the second envelope. It was fine paper. I slid my finger under the flap, and opened it.

> *Dear Mrs. Spencer:*
> *You haven't answered my recent correspondence, perhaps due*
> *to the aberrations of the U.S. Mail in the West. I trust that*
> *no ill fortune has befallen you, or your anonymous friend who*
> *authored the stories you sent me. Let me assure you that these*
> *stories have been very well received by our public. While they don't*
> *have the raw savagery of a Ned Buntline, they capture the travails*
> *of a feminine presence on the frontier, without bawdy houses or*
> *excesses of a romantic nature. Our readership among young girls*
> *has greatly increased in the three issues in which Martha Moody*
> *has appeared, and I would like to contract for six more stories*
> *immediately.*

Now I must broach the matter of payment and authorship. I am enclosing a cheque made out to the Bearer for the stories I have published. I trust that the sum will be found sufficient. I did not disturb your friend's anonymity, of course, since you did not give me her name. I attributed the stories to "A Woman of the West." Her identity has excited interest among our readers, but our employees have been instructed to reveal nothing. I, however, would like to correspond with her to offer my admiration and confirm our contract. I leave these arrangements in your good hands.

Warm Regards,
Frank Sibsen, Editor and Publisher
True Western Tales

I looked at the check. "Seventy-five dollars" was written two ways across its face. I folded the check and the letter back into its thick ivory-colored envelope and closed it in the Bible. Then I tucked the book under my arm, picked up my sunbonnet, and went out to find Miss Alice.

I dragged a bale of hay into the sunshine and talked to her while she grazed. I said I didn't want Martha swimming in trousers in front of a magazine world. Miss Alice swatted flies. I asked her if she had ever read *True Western Tales.* Miss Alice didn't look up, but took a few slow-hoofed steps into the thicker grass. I knew Clara must get it, but it would get to Moody months after they were reading each issue in the East. I felt a burning on my neck and slapped a midge. Miss Alice stared at me and considered skittering away like a calf.

"Miss Alice," I said, "we'd have to sell a ton of butter before we made seventy-five dollars." The backs of my legs prickled against the hay. "They don't have my name."

I sat there a long time, scratching my ankle and trying to feel something simple. Miss Alice wandered away, then came back to snatch some hay. I decided to look to the words of the prophets, and opened the Bible to God raining meat on the greedy children of Israel, who had seen rivers pour from the rock when they were thirsty and asked for a table in the wilderness. God is angry that his wonders are taken so lightly, so he gives them what they ask for, then kills the fattest as they eat.

I read aloud for Miss Alice. "He rained flesh also upon them as dust, and feathered fowls like as the sand of the sea."

Just then, I saw dust rising in the road. It was Ruth coming back with the groceries, but I could see who she had with her even from this far down the road. I thought of running into the barn, but I never knew if John might be hiding there himself, so in the end I just kept sitting on the bale of hay, watching the small girl and the big man come closer and closer. When I could make out the gold watch chain gleaming on his chest, I got up and walked through the yard to meet them halfway between the house and the road.

"Afternoon, Mrs. Linger," said Charles Balm, shifting his load of groceries to tip his hat.

"Put those sacks on the ground, then get." I was a long way past politeness. I reached through my skirt pocket and put my hand on my knife.

Ruth put her sack down. She was about to run off, but I grabbed her by one sleeve. "Wait," I told her. "Be ready to run, but don't leave us alone."

Martha's father put his sack down next to the other one. "That's no way to talk. I was doing you a favor, carrying these potatoes all the way out here."

The girl was kicking the dirt, and I let go of her. She shoved her hands in her pockets and looked miserable. I felt sorry for her, but I needed her to stay. She was protection.

"What do you want?" I kept a blade's length between me and Mr. Balm.

He spoke as if he were leading a Sunday School class. "Why, I'm simply a concerned neighbor. I heard that you had moved out of Clara Spencer's, and you hadn't been into the store for so long, I thought you might be sick." He took a step towards Ruth, who skipped back. "I couldn't get a word out of this girl, so I decided I'd better come see for myself."

The girl opened her mouth, and I noticed that she had a chip the shape of a crescent moon out of her front left tooth. "I didn't say, Mrs. Linger. He guessed."

"That's true," said Mr. Balm, "although why I had to guess is another question."

I stomped my foot on the grass. One of the sacks of groceries fell on its side, and a potato rolled out. "I like my privacy."

Mr. Balm picked up the potato and handed it to me with a bow. I took it. "Martha doesn't speak of you," he said, watching my face, "but she misses you."

He was trying to read my expression, but I didn't give him a flicker. I suddenly knew that I was safe, that he was not going to molest me. He had walked all the way out here to study my eyes while he said his daughter's name. He suspected she had feelings for me, and he thought I would show him how deep they might be.

I pointed the potato at the sky. "It's about to rain," I said. "You had better go."

The girl took off across the fields, running so fast that she left no trail in the grasses. She was running towards chores and supper under the clouds that I had brought on as if by will.

Martha's father looked at me for a moment longer, fingering his watch chain. He seemed unsatisfied, but he touched his hat. "I won't think of doing you a favor again, Mrs. Linger. Good day."

I carried the sacks of food into the house, and was dumping the potatoes in the root cellar when the storm broke. Water would be rolling off him all the way back to town. I stood in the doorway watching the sheets of rain and thinking of a woman whose hips could beat clouds into butter. He said she never spoke of me.

That night I wrote Martha in the wilderness. She was lost on the plains at night. Her hair was loose around her shoulders, and the wind swept her skirt out behind her. She was walking slowly across the flat ground. The grasses rustled. The stars pulsed above her. She didn't reckon by the dim North Star, but followed bright Venus, whose position shifted against the fixed stars.

She was trying to find water.

I made her desperate, so thirsty that her throat had closed up to all except the thinnest stream of dry air. Even in the cool of night, her skin burned. She had her fat to draw on, but her mind was dull. She stumbled on and on with her eyes on Venus until it set. Martha kept walking, looking for a thicker darkness that might be a stand of trees.

She heard a buzz. She walked with the noise for a while before she felt the first bite. Then she was deep in a cloud of mosquitoes as thirsty as she was. They landed on her neck and her wrists and bit through her dress. She slapped at them frantically, but as many as she killed found a place on her to fill up with blood. Martha was losing her last wetness. She drew her shawl up over her face for protection, but she soon stumbled over a rock and fell. She lay curled on the ground, swatting and cursing, until she heard another low sound that brought her back to her feet. It was moving water.

I fell asleep in the chair as Martha drank.

Nine

The next morning I sat down in the sunlight at my kitchen table and wrote a letter to Frank Sibsen, editor and publisher. I told him my name and accepted his payment. I said that I preferred to remain A Woman of the West to his readers, and I asked that he change the name of my protagonist. I went through my roll of stories and picked five—the one where she braided the wolf's tail, the one where she found the diamond cave—only I crossed out Martha Moody and wrote in Bella Jones every time her name appeared.

When I finished, I put the letter and the stories in an envelope, and ate another one of the biscuits that I had made with the flour from town. I listened as I always did for a strain of horn music, but all I heard were the loud morning birds. For a moment I missed John coming in with his muddy boots and bright hair to appreciate my cooking and pray with me before breakfast. He'd be eating a plateful of these biscuits thick with Miss Alice's sweet butter. But then the old wave of tension washed over me, and I closed my eyes and fought to calm myself with the knowledge there was no certainty of seeing him today, or any morning. That had to be progress. I wiped the crumbs from my mouth and got to work.

———

I was pumping water when I realized I had to tell Martha about the stories, not the next time I saw her, but now. The water spilled over the lip of the pail and wet my brick-red skirt. I stopped pumping and looked down the dusty road, then decided to take the shortcut through the fields.

I hurried back to the house to find the envelope with my note to the editor and the Bella Jones stories. I slipped it into a pocket of my skirt. I took off John's jacket and brushed my hair, then took the water to Miss Alice and poured it in her trough. She looked at me, then lowered her head for a drink.

I scratched her neck. "I'm going to town, Miss Alice."

I walked to the back gate, and she followed, chewing her cud and plodding along as if prepared to walk behind me for a very long way. I turned around and pushed her nose to one side. "No."

She took two steps closer. I could feel her breath on my arm. I pushed her again. "No, Miss Alice. I'm not leaving for good. I'll be back in a couple of hours."

She bared her yellow teeth and bawled as if I were taking her calf to auction. I scratched between her ears and opened the gate. She watched as I latched it behind me. I patted her nose through the fence and talked softly to her about town and trains and crinolines, as if she were a small child I was putting down for a nap. She bawled again when I finally turned my back and took the path that boys and dogs had worn through the high grasses.

The trail steered clear of houses, which suited me. I was agitated, uncertain of what I would say to Martha. She would be in the middle of her work day, with her father nearby. Martha had whispered sonnets with her lips against my cheek, but I had never told her that I wrote by the fire at night. I had never spoken of such things to anyone. I had been afraid that she would laugh, or that she would ask to read them.

I had never spoken to Martha of her body, either, but I had written of her breasts falling in cascades of fat and nipple over her padded ribs. I had never mentioned her hips because I didn't want her to think me indecent, but I had written that their motion churned the sky. Clara had read words too private for my lover's ears.

I was most scared to tell Martha that I'd written her into a hero, as if who she was weren't enough. She had puffy eyes and a cold streak when she was tired. I knew she pandered to her father. I loved her with accurate passion. I had seen the rash under Martha's breasts, but I had also seen that her hair was red foam, her knees were dimpled and her fists were tight. She had poured water over my feet as if I were Christ, and there was no part of me that could forget that.

I had changed under the water and under her hands to a woman with a voice. I began to speak. It was inspiration. She brought me to sex and to voice. She gave me a mouthful of wine. I drank. I put my tongue along her tensed lips.

The way I felt when I was moving words was so close to what she gave me with her knee between my legs. She was mammoth. She haunted me. Since I was lost to God, my soul was my own, but when I wrote I found Martha, the miracle, riding a golden cow.

I wanted my words seen. I wanted Martha to be in the vision of the world, with her low-slung belly swaying in the morning of a culture. Martha, the adamant vision: the woman standing on the scalloped shell emerging from the sea.

I walked quickly along the narrow path. The wind picked up. I skirted Clara's land. I was hurrying, breathing hard, and felt almost lost in the stretch of sky and the dry gold grasses rustling against my hips. I was walking towards Martha, in dread of losing everything she was to me because I had written her name, but the grass and the wind were courting me: touching my arms, twisting stems to show me both sides of a seed head, parting to offer me a place to step off the path and float through the grasses as I would on a deep stream. I pulled a blade of grass, and split its white end with my thumbnail as I walked.

The wind came over the grasses at me. My skirt blew against my legs. I heard the song of a bird. It was repetitive and sweet. The stalks left seed on the wet skirt of my dress.

I came into the shelter of the hill that hid Clara's house from view, and the wind calmed. I pushed my hair back into its bun. A snake crossed the path, sinuous, alert. I watched it disappear. It had a pattern of linked diamonds on its back.

My dread had hardened into a sourball like the kind Martha sold out of glass boxes in her counter. I picked some red clover and chewed the leaves.

The hill sloped away from me. Every edge of grass on its surface was in motion. I thought of Martha's breast moving under my hands. As I rounded the hill and the wind hit me full again, I stopped. I looked back up at the grasses shivering on the gentle rise. It was dirt and roots and green in the wind.

I didn't have to be looking through Martha at it. I could see it myself. The hill curved like Martha's breasts, and I had sat on the other side of it leaning against her in front of Clara's windows, but the shape had been there, shifting slowly, before either of us had been born. I had once believed that the strength of the hills was the Lord's. Now when I saw the grasses shaking in the wind, they shook me to joy. It was quick. The dread that

I had been sucking melted. My ears ached, but I could hear my heart.

I looked my fill, then walked on. It wasn't much farther to town. The joy left, but I felt shaped different, as if I couldn't contain things in the same way since I'd let the shape of the hill curve into my eyes. The path took a turn towards the road. I was almost to town, where Martha might forgive me or not.

As I walked into Moody, a wagon pulled past me on the road. The horse was old and slow. The bearded man holding the reins nodded gravely. He was hauling a load of children, who were punching each other's arms and throwing handfuls of feathers out the back of the wagon. I recognized the girl Ruth as she swung an empty feed sack at one of the boys in overalls. He grabbed it out of her hand when she stopped to stare at me.

When I got to Moody's, the boys were on the porch. Ruth and the farmer were nowhere to be seen. The smallest was bent over to kiss Martha's cat, Bathsheba, his overalls gaping open to show his skinny ribs. I could see Mr. Balm in the window, standing behind the cash register with his thumbs hooked in his vest.

The boys pushed open the door. I stood on the porch behind them. I heard them saying rock candy, birch beer, Buffalo Bill. I knelt down next to the cat and rubbed her warm side. She purred, and I felt absolved of throwing her in Mr. Balm's face. I looked through the plate-glass window, between the two Os in MOODY'S, as Mr. Balm stared at the boys, watching their hands as they walked up and down the candy aisle. He picked up a feather duster and followed.

I took my chance and walked into the store. The little brass bells in the doorway jingled over my head. I marched down the center aisle, past the barrels of beans and grain and the onion bin and bolts of cloth, with my cheeks burning and my head full of the time Martha and I had walked slowly across the back of the store with her finger inside me. She had caressed my legs as we climbed the stairs. At each stair I had stopped and pushed back against the ledge of her breasts as she climbed behind me.

Her office door was closed, but the light showed through the yellow glass panel with OFFICE painted on it in gilt. I knocked, then turned the knob. Mr. Balm hadn't seen me. I heard a boy say, "Corset stays make great pea shooters."

Martha looked up from her desk. I saw grief loose in her cheeks before they tightened and gladdened. I shut the door behind me, and stood out of view of the glass. She rose and walked over to me. "Amanda. How good to see you. But what are you doing here?" I remembered the shape of that hill, and took a deep breath. "I wrote about you."

Martha put her hand to the jet buttons on the front of her dress. "What?"

I lost the hill, reached, and ran my palms over the buttons. Martha leaned into my hands and said, "I don't understand."

I wanted to keep her leaning towards me and wondering what I had to tell her, but I answered. "I've been writing about you every night. I have to, or I can't sleep." I let my hands slip down the black silk over her hips, then I took them away.

Martha smoothed her dress after the path of my hands. "You never told me."

I brushed grass seed from my skirt. "I was embarrassed. In some of the stories I pretended things."

"What things?" She folded her big arms and waited.

"That you could fly. That you spoke with cows and angels." Martha looked astonished, then she burst out laughing so loud that I was afraid her father would come. She put her arm around my waist. "You're silly."

I wished I could be relieved. "I know, Martha. I was just playing."

She wiped her eyes, still smiling. "Are you going to show me any of these stories?"

I had the envelope for Frank Sibsen, editor, in my skirt pocket, but I didn't reach for it. It was so natural to touch and flirt after having been without each other. I wanted to relax into it, to pull out a story and read her something dangerous about her breasts and the ways her hips moved. Instead, I kept talking. "John found the stories. He's forgotten them, maybe, but that's why he hurt me that day in the barn. Then Clara found them under the mattress when I was staying with her. She sent some of them to a magazine."

"Damnation!" Martha slammed her fist against her thigh, and I was watching the rows of jet buttons shake when her father pounded on the door.

"Martha, let me in! This can't wait." Mr. Balm's voice thundered like he was a preacher.

"I don't want him to see you." Martha and I looked at each other, then she stepped to the desk and shoved her chair out of the way. "Hide."

I granted her that. I crouched under the desk while she went to open the door. I heard her father step into the room, saw his shiny boots surrounded by bare feet. The boys were with him, and they were jumping with excitement.

"Here she is, on the front, this is her."

"Martha Moody," declaimed her father, "Belle of the West. Martha, you're on the cover of a yellow pulp magazine."

I could feel Martha's panic. It shook the slatted floor. Her skirt blocked my view as she stood in front of the desk. I wanted to reach under it and rub her calf to comfort her, but I knew better than to try it.

The boys kept squealing. "It's you, Mrs. Moody. It's you. It's you. It's your name, plain as anything."

Martha's tight voice cut through theirs. "It must be another Moody, father."

Cramped in the dust under the desk, I felt a sudden pride. It wasn't another Moody, it was my love, and even boys would see her big and real and fast-moving as a train.

He was turning the pages slowly, a careful man. "A cow with wings walks into her store. They fly through the sky together. That's quite a coincidence, another Martha Moody with red hair and a store."

Martha sounded only slightly irritated, but her hem rippled with tension. "I haven't read it. I don't know what it says, but I find it hard to believe that I have been featured in a penny dreadful without my knowledge."

"Yes," said Martha's father. "It does boggle the mind."

The boys caught the strain in the talk between the Moodys and stopped jumping and screeching. One crossed his feet. Two backed towards the door. One stepped up to the shiny boots. "Sir, can I buy the magazine?"

Martha shifted her weight. "I'd like to read it."

"We have extra issues." Her father no longer sounded like a preacher of the prophets. He was muttering at her. "They sent us fifty extra of this number. I thought it was an error." His voice snaked down to me. "Are you sure you know nothing about this, Martha?"

Her skirt was hanging straight and still. "Who is the author? Is it a person we know?"

The pages snapped as her father flicked them. "Here it is," he said. "The author signs herself, 'A Woman of the West.'"

"How very brave," said Martha, "to use my name and not her own." I cringed.

"Or his own," said her father in his smoothest voice. "With a pseudonym, one can't assume."

The boy said to Martha, "Will you sign it, Ma'am?" I could hear the clinks as he played with the coins in his hands.

She sighed, then her skirt stretched as she put one foot upon a rung of her chair and signed the magazine on her knee. It whirred like a bird as she tossed it through the air to him. He clapped his hands together to catch it with a smack, then the bare feet ran out of the room.

Mr. Balm spoke softly. "You're a cheap story any boy can buy for a nickel. Thank God you have Moody's name, and not mine."

The boys ran back into the room, their dirty feet dancing around Martha's skirt. "Sign mine, Mrs. Moody, will you? Sign this one."

Martha scratched with her pen. "You may say what you wish, father, but I'm a woman of business, and this magazine seems to be good for trade."

Martha barely spoke to me when she locked her office door behind her father, and I crawled out from under her desk. She sat leafing through *True Western Tales* while I stood very close to her and whispered urgently about John's addled mind and how I had left Clara's house when I discovered what she had done. I told Martha how it had felt, sitting by the stove night after night, pretending to mend until John was asleep, then pulling out my paper and building her in my lap, giving her words, giving her deeds, giving her every grace she already had, working intently in the only live corner of my night. I hadn't spoken of this to her in the mornings at the store because I hadn't known how to speak. This moment, as I whispered in her ear, was my first attempt to tell a complicated truth. I told Martha this, and she moved her hand across the cheap paper of the magazine. She wasn't even reading. I think she was trying to absorb it by feel.

I kept talking. I told her that I thought the world spoke to her by its physical qualities. She heard the store with its pickles and teas and sanded counter because it spoke to her. So did the cold hug of water, and my tart body. So did some Shakespeare and certain biblical passages with their explicit oils and plants and blisters. But she had known the smell and the feel of her big leather Shakespeare well before she had gone into its words, and now the ink of *True Western Tales* was smudging on her fingers as I talked.

I told her I wrote about her after John had read the stories because I had a pressure inside me. I wrote about her because I was without her company and she had first brought me to words and passion. That was enough of a miracle, but I made her fly and jump mountains because she was something immense to me, and I was trying to say what she was.

Martha might have been listening, or she might have been waiting with hate in her heart. I couldn't tell by her face or the slow movements of her hands turning and smoothing the pages of the magazine.

I took a deep breath, then I told her more. I told her about combing Miss Alice, reading the Bible and worrying about the empty cellar. I didn't say how much I had needed her day after day. I told her about the letter and the check, and how her father had come out with the groceries. I didn't tell her how he had touched me in the store. I was exhausting myself with this burst of truth, and had taken it about as far as I could bear. I told her about changing the name to Bella, but I didn't mention that the envelope addressed to the editor was still in my pocket. I couldn't give that up.

I did tell her about the wind and the small seeds sticking to my skirt as I walked to her, and how I had looked at a hill and thought it was beautiful in its own right, with a separate power as strong as sex, as strong as hers.

Martha came to the end of *True Western Tales* and put her hands flat on the desk. My voice trailed off.

"Are you done?" she asked.

I nodded. She got up and walked to the office door. "I'll lock this from the outside and let you out when my father is upstairs."

I waited, depleted and without thought through the hours until she came back, then I slipped past her silent figure and her goods, and stumbled out the door. I took a deep breath in the sun before I hurried down the dry road to the post office to send more stories into the world.

When I came out of the post office, Theda Wilks and her friend Dora Hassett were out strolling the boardwalk with parasols. Dora nodded and Theda stared at me with one hand to her mouth. I clasped my own hands in front of me and nodded back. Their heads pulled close together after they passed me. I crossed Main Street and walked towards the train station, wondering whether they were talking about the last time Theda had seen me, when I had just thrown a cat in Mr. Balm's face, or my general state as a woman abandoned by her husband walking through town with grass and carpet dust on her dress.

I ducked into the station to get out of the public eye. The station master didn't look up from the novel he was reading behind the ticket grille. The air smelled of varnished wood benches, old sweat and fried potatoes. I thought of sitting down in hard comfort to gather my thoughts, but then I saw a man stretched out on one of the corner benches as if he'd been there for hours. It was my sleeping husband, John.

He was turned on his side facing the wall, so I couldn't see his face, but I could see his spine making a knobbed edge under the linen; he was very thin. The shirt looked clean. Pink patches of scalp shone through his hair. His horn stood bell down on the floor beside the bench.

I forced myself to keep walking quietly through the station and out to the train platform. Carry A. Nation had stood there and urged Christian women to smash. I jumped off the platform and began to follow the tracks.

I went west from Moody, walking alongside the rails in short grasses. My skirt rustled. I threw out my arms, agitated, excited, aware of my squat figure following the tracks into the stretch of grasses and sky. The wind blew dirt on my teeth. I was giddy with seeing Martha and John and Clara's hill, with the squalor of my human ties, with the big check and the stories in the mail. It was all too much for me. I lifted my red skirt and swirled it above my knees.

Then I saw the little girl. She was lying on her back on the tracks, waving her hands over her head and kicking her feet in the air. Her purple calico dress was blown flat against her. Then she rolled on her stomach and pretended to be sighting a rifle down the tracks towards town, straight at me.

"Get her!" she yelled over her shoulder, then she started crawling on her belly over the hot rails, making sputtering noises like bullets of air.

"Hello, Ruth," I said. She reached my feet, and aimed her imaginary rifle at my face. I offered her a hand, and she stood up.

"You were dancing," she said, brushing the dust from the front of her dress. "I saw your knees."

I pushed the hair out of my eyes. "You were flailing. That's as bad."

She slung her invisible rifle over her shoulder, and fell into step beside me. "I'm a child."

I pulled a grass blade for a whistle. "You're a girl."

She felt in her pocket and brought out a big handkerchief with an embroidered violet losing its stitches in one corner. "Why bring that up?" She blew her nose.

I wiped mine on my sleeve. "Ruth, I need a favor."

"Blow?" She offered me her handkerchief. I shook my head. "What favor?"

"Run into town and buy me the latest copy of *True Western Tales.* Buy yourself something too, and don't tell anyone who it's for."

"A sasparilla," said Ruth, counting my coins, "plus one bonbon."

"Hurry. I'll wait here for you." I watched Ruth run back towards Moody with her air-slicing stride, then I sat down beside the track to wait. I felt exhausted. Every grass across the plain was in motion. Only the track was still and solid, and I rested my eyes on its lines.

Ruth came back with a chocolate moustache and a red magazine. She handed it over. "A bunch of kids were buying this because Martha Moody is in it."

The cowgirl on the cover was swinging a lariat and riding a winged beast that looked more like a deer than a cow, but the words said: FEATURING MARTHA MOODY, BELLE OF THE WEST.

"She doesn't look anything like our Martha Moody, except for the red hair." Ruth shrugged.

I folded the magazine under my arm and thanked Ruth, who saluted me as I walked away. I crossed my eyes at her, then waved and headed home.

I waited to read it until I got to the house, then forgot to close the door behind me because I was in such a rush to open the magazine.

It began "One day an angel was walking down the main street of Moody. She saw a store and entered. A stout, redheaded woman was behind the counter. . ."

It was my story, the first one I had written after I had lost temperance and found Martha's bed. The editor had changed "breast" to "bosom" but Martha was still fat and the angel was a cow, just as I had written it. The skinny cowgirl and her lariat were nowhere to be found. It read like a child's fantasy, with Martha dancing the sky into cream like the story from my childhood of the giant who made it thunder when potatoes fell out of his cart.

I read it three times through, then I took it out to the barn and read it aloud to Miss Alice. I gave her some grain, and milked her while she listened.

"That's you, Miss Alice. You're the angel. There's not yellow lightning on your udders, but you are otherwise a buttery cow."

I stood up with the bucket and the story, and patted her on the flank. She bent her neck to look at me and blew grass-scented breath on my hand.

We were both turning red and purple with the sunset that was pouring in the open barn door. I felt lonely, washed with color, almost hopeful. Miss Alice yawned and showed her yellow teeth.

"People read this," I told her. "Boys shovel out barns to earn enough to buy it."

Miss Alice raised her tail, and I carried the bucket out of the barn. "Martha doesn't like it," I said from the door. The sun was down, but still giving colored light.

Miss Alice lay down, so I stopped talking. I put her milk on the shelf for the cream to rise. I walked through the dark to the house, and went quickly to sleep.

Ten

I was relieved to go back to my work in the days that followed. I planted beans, collards and squash in the garden, using the water I saved by not scalding my linens to coax the plants into leaf. I baked bread and biscuits and sweet rolls whose crust broke on my lips before I bit into them. Miss Alice seemed to be slowing down on our walks across the pasture, but she was giving more milk than I could drink. Ruth had brought me a new paddle for my churn, so I could make butter again. I was extravagant with myself, coloring the butter with carrot juice and working it into pretty balls stamped with milk pitchers and roses. Once I molded half a churning into a plate-shaped round so that I could butter a whole cornbread with one cut. I was attentive to the butter so it was smooth and rich as honey, but I knew better than to try to sell it at the store.

Ruth had taken to stopping by almost every day, so I gave her milk and butter to take home to her family. It was a sin to waste it, and I liked how she spent time with Miss Alice, tracing the curly hair on the cow's forehead or clambering up on her back to whisper in her ear. Miss Alice didn't seem to mind, and I was glad to have the company. I gave her balls of butter stamped with a bolt of lightning, and hired her to do my shopping.

I paid her in nickels and butter. She would show up at the barn at milking time, a sharp-chinned girl in a plain dress, sitting on the edge of the trough and feeding handfuls of oats to Miss Alice. I was surprised to see her so early at first, then I learned to have my list and my money with me when I went out to the barn at dawn.

"Don't you have to help your mother with her chores in the mornings?"

"Naw, she doesn't miss me. Besides, she likes the butter."

Ruth would take off running while the sun was still yawning, and come back down the road from Moody before dark, hugging sacks full of my supplies. I didn't ask her any questions. She minded her business and loved Miss Alice, so we got along.

I thought about theological questions and stopped combing my hair. I stayed away from water, except what I needed for Miss Alice and the garden. I went through all my clothes and all of John's that would fit me, then started over without setting a fire under the pot for a wash.

I had spent years cumbered about with serving, careful and troubled about the canning and linens, so now I wanted to sit at the foot of Clara's hill and let the grasses give me the part of life which was not earned, but chosen. I thought of myself as having been immersed in falseness, and washing now seemed like a danger to me: an exposure or loss. I let my body's dirt be. There was no one to see me but Ruth, who said nothing.

I was very lonely, but the stories were still coming in bursts. I carried paper in my apron pocket so I could write down every scene as it came to me:

Men were sitting on the porch of Moody's store one night, debating about the sacred. The Reverend was off at the swimming hole, where he liked to go alone at night, so he wasn't there to embarrass the discussion, and somehow things had drifted away from schisms and got hung on the nature of God.

The men chewed tobacco and leaned on the cracker barrel, serious. The sheriff said he believed the laws of nature and science were expressions of a Higher Mind. The blacksmith sat on a railing, drumming his hands on his thighs and calling out, "Sweet Jesus!" The banker didn't like his rhythmic way with the Lord's name, and said such matters were best left in church. He stubbed his cigar out in the dust, and crossed Main Street by moonlight.

When a farmer said God was a father, a ram, not a pasty-faced lamb-kisser from colored pictures, the sheriff sent a boy into the store to fetch Martha.

He bowed from the waist as she stepped onto the porch. "I'll keep watch on the cash register, Ma'am. There are mortal matters to discuss."

Martha stood in the doorway with her hands stuck in the pocket of her black apron. She looked around the circle of men's faces in the silver light. Ruth was chasing June bugs within voice range. She and Martha were the only human females out that night.

The sheriff posed the question, fingering his badge. "Mrs. Moody, you are familiar with mysteries. I've heard that you've spoken with water and had it speak back. Could you give us an image of God we could care about?"

Martha pulled a pipe from her pocket and lit it. The smoke smelled fruity and sharp. "Why ask me? I'm just here to sell mops and cream."

The men coughed and shifted. They knew she had powers. The blacksmith started stomping his boots on the porch, and they all picked it up.

The sheriff tensed and raised his hand. "Now, we've all been making purchases from Mrs. Moody for years. Show some respect." He gave every point of the circle his magnetic election-day eye, and the stomping died off.

Martha smiled and breathed smoke. It looked yellow so near the lantern, and drifted over the men like a butter fog.

They all heard the slow clop of cloven hooves on sawdust as Azreal walked out through the store. The sheriff stood aside, his mouth gaping. The cow had her wings folded across her back. She ambled over to Martha, leaned against her, and lifted her muzzle to Martha's ear. "Tell them to take off their golden earrings and bring them to you."

The cow shone with a cold light that cast Martha's shadow over the porch and to the edge of Main Street. The men huddled together, but the sheriff stepped up and tapped Martha on the shoulder. "Um, Ma'am. None of us wear earrings. If you could wait for us to go home and talk to our wives, we could come up with a pile of gold, I'd guarantee." The sheriff was a bachelor, but confident.

Just then, a great rattling began. All metal started to move. Every watch and gun was shaking on the man that wore it. The blacksmith screamed. His glasses were dancing above him, floating over his face like a big-eyed silver spider. The sheriff's badge pounded and buckled on his chest. His guns rose and clicked their butts like castanets. Pennies and half dollars spun on the boards. Belt buckles dragged men behind them across the ground. Men tangled in each other's spurs.

There was no noise from the pots and axes and shovels inside the store. Ruth crouched in the darkness with the June bugs, who were whirring and clicking as on any other night.

A squirming pile of men fell off the porch, stuck together by the metal on their persons. They knocked the cracker barrel off, too, and it splintered. Crackers shaped like hearts and eyes and silhouettes scattered in the dust.

"Listen!" shouted Martha from the cleared porch, "this is an old story."

Azreal looked at Martha standing on the edge of the porch with her hands raised and her red hair catching lantern light from the back. "You're a fine figure of a woman," said the cow. "Let's wrestle."

The men shouted and thrashed in their pile on the ground. Azreal and Martha circled each other. Suddenly the cow brought one of her wings forward and slashed across Martha's skirt. The cloth split, and Martha jumped back. Then she grinned and threw herself on Azreal's broad, muscled neck.

"Careful!" yelled Ruth, drawing closer to the porch. Some of the men were cursing and some were listening to what was happening on the porch.

Martha held the angel's neck close to her shoulders trying to tussle her to the ground. Azreal beat her wings, making a wind that loosed Martha's hair from its bun and blew her ripped skirt up over her petticoat. Martha didn't loosen her grasp, but took a step closer and wrapped one foot around Azreal's foreleg. The cow lifted her hoof and stomped. The boards of the porch splintered beneath her, but Martha held on.

Sweat poured from the woman's face like wax from a hot candle. She grunted, then dropped her full weight on the cow's neck. The two figures fell to the buckling surface of the porch, and writhed: the cow on her back, hooves and wings in the air; the woman with her black-stockinged legs wrapped around the cow's golden sides, flopping and groaning and clinging to the animal with all her might. Azreal contracted her wings, then she used their feathered muscles to lift her from her back and push off from the porch. They hung low in the air while Martha struggled to straddle the cow's back, then they rose and flew toward the moon, laughing and breathing hard and whipping up a wind behind them.

The men found that they could untangle themselves, and they went home with whatever guns and watches they found stuck in their pockets. The next day they sorted through their possessions and fixed the porch for Martha. The sheriff asked Ruth who had won the wrestling match, but she just chewed on her fingers and said she didn't know. Martha opened the store three days later, looking like a proper laced-up matron. No one asked her about mysteries after that. It was dangerous.

I braved town whenever I had stories to send to Frank Sibsen of *True Western Tales*. He had agreed to accept mail from me at a post office box and sign my checks in his bookkeeper's name so no one in Moody could trace them back to the magazine, but he had balked at changing my character's name to Bella Jones.

He had used great flourishes of ink to write me that she was already too well-known as Martha Moody, especially among the young girls who were starting to subscribe to the magazine in large numbers for the first time.

I myself had tried to remember to write "Bella" every time I thought "Martha," but it was no use. Martha had stamped her name on my stories. I told myself that the damage from using her name had already been done, and kept sending them out.

People stared at me in town, especially the women who used to sit with me on church committees, but I didn't want to give Ruth my packets full of stories to mail. She was too sharp and they were too mysterious. I tried to remember to put on a bonnet and change into a dark dress before I went to town, but then I would forget that I was wearing John's big boots until I had tromped mud on the post office floor.

I didn't stop at Moody's Store, of course, but I looked at the windows as I passed. One afternoon the poster selling Pear's Soap was gone, and in its place was a white placard with red lettering that announced, "Home of MARTHA MOODY. Signed photographs, one nickel." There was a framed photograph of Martha next to it, dressed like the model from the cover of *True Western Tales*, with a lasso in her lap. There was a cast-iron rack on the porch, with the last few numbers of the magazine displayed: MARTHA MOODY—FEAR ON BUZZARD'S CLIFF. MARTHA MOODY IN THE FLOODED CREEK. I shivered. Frank had been sending me the issues as they appeared, but I had never seen them on public display before, much less on Martha's porch. I remembered her standing under this awning sipping from a goblet the day Carry Nation had come to town. I caught a glimpse of her father standing next to the cash register, staring out over the aisles, so I hurried on.

I did my business at the post office and headed out of town, but I couldn't stop thinking of that photograph. I felt like a hypocrite, but I was shocked that Martha was selling costumed photographs. Lillie Langtry appeared in soap advertisements, but she was a professional beauty from London. Martha was not. I wondered if she had read all of the stories, and what she thought of them. Clara had done a good job of picking the innocent ones, but I always saw my body's memories in the character of Martha, whether she was touching an apple or riding the winged cow through the sky. I wondered if the real Martha felt it, too, or if she just saw something cheap and silly for children. I had made it past the outskirts of town when I looked up and saw Theda Wilks riding towards me on her mare. If I could have turned off the road and disappeared into the fields, I would have, but the flat land offered no cover, so I kept walking and hoped she wouldn't speak. There was no one else on the road.

Theda had gloves on her big hands. She lifted the reins with one finger and her horse came to a clipped stop. Theda had a way with horseflesh and beautiful carriage in the saddle. I straightened my own back and gave her a nod.

"Amanda Linger, you're dirty." Theda waved her hands in the air above me as I passed her. Her horse stood alert and stockstill. "Have you lost all Christian decency?"

I shrugged and kept walking, but my face burned. I had always admired Theda. She was blunt and rich and elegant. She had smashed a full-length nude in the saloon and worn an axe to church.

She turned her horse to look after me. "We pray for you."

I stopped and breathed the dust I'd kicked up, then turned to face her. I thought I was going to thank her with quiet sarcasm, I thought I was just tucking the long tail of John's shirt, but my hands had grown bolder since I had been on my own, and they pulled the shirt tails out of my waistband and lifted them to show Theda my white belly there in the public road.

Theda looked at me impassively, as if she were made of salt. Then she tensed her fingers and her mare stepped into a trot. They circled me. Theda said, "You're a lunatic," then headed into town.

I didn't bother to tuck in my shirt, but let it flap the whole way home.

The less time I spent on keeping myself, the more I groomed Miss Alice. That afternoon I stood beside her with the curry comb, and told her how I could feel the eyes on me in town, how Theda had commented, how others whispered or hissed. I felt uneasy in Moody, and I knew it wasn't just my new lax habits, but some fundamental change in me that was easy for their eyes to mark.

Miss Alice bent to eat grass, and I ran the comb over her muscled neck. "Passion shouldn't have happened to me, and I'm not prepared for grace. I had enough work with scrubbing the floor and bleaching John's shirts and ironing them stiff with starch. I was always boiling water. I had religious zeal and temperance to fight for, and Clara Spencer for spice and gossip and the motions of friendship. I had you for milk and butter and sour cream. I was a decent woman. I was plain. Why was Martha desperate enough to touch my legs?"

Miss Alice didn't like me to mess with her tail, and ran a yard or two away from me when I tried to tease out the burrs. I had to chase her down, still talking. "She made me tremble. She touched my body tenderly. She was soft and her waist fell and folded into mine. She gathered my belly in her hands, she rubbed her cheek on my small breasts, she pushed her loose breasts against my loose hips, and we were soft in mounds and extravagant in flesh."

Miss Alice finally stood still for me to get the last burrs. She looked clean and almost glossy, but flies hovered near her face. She licked her nose with her long, pale tongue and lowered her head to nudge me.

"Eat grass," I said, pushing back. "No oats." I cleaned the hair out of the curry comb and dropped it to catch in the flowering weeds. "What do they see on me in town that they don't see on Martha?"

I heard an answer in my head, apt but incomplete: Martha washes.

The next morning Ruth came running across the pasture just as I finished the milking. She helped me carry that day's churning to the house, then sat down outside on the stone step that John and I had dug from the earth with so much work.

I had taken to writing in the mornings before I baked and churned, but Ruth sat on the step picking at scabs on her knees and chattering until I came out and sat down beside her.

I wasn't sure how it had happened. Ruth had always seemed tough to me, but that morning she was looking at me and the world with big clear eyes like a cow, so I was drawn out into the morning sun and started talking stories to her like I would to Miss Alice when I was milking.

I must have still been burning from what Theda had said, because I started in with the story of Jezebel, whose name had come to mean a harlot and a woman to shun. I didn't tell it strictly as I got it from Kings, but I did let Ruth know that Jezebel ate the food left in sacrifice to idols and may have caused the death of many who stood against her. The point that caught me, the thing that made it worth telling, though, was how Jezebel, with her armies defeated and her son dead, sat near a window in her fancy house. She sat there breathing scented air as she had all her life, and she prayed to spirits she found more responsive than one jealous Lord. Then she put on a scarlet silk dress. She painted her lips red and lined her eyes with kohl. She attired her hair with scarves and precious stones and pearls and sat by the window looking out.

I showed her to Ruth, sitting high above the street, holding her chin up, no longer powerful, but adorned. I knew her painted face did her no good. Her own eunuchs threw her out of that window, and she was trampled by her enemy's horse. In the Bible, dogs eat all of her body, except for her skull and her feet and the palms of her hands. But I couldn't say that to Ruth, who sat next to me with her hands on her knees, chewing on a piece of her own hair, so I told her that when Jezebel saw her enemy's horses raising dust in the road, she jumped. She jumped from that window wearing all of her best clothes, and landed on a pack of wild dogs, who pressed their thin bodies close to each other so that they could carry her out of the city on their backs.

Jezebel lived with the dogs in a den in the hills, and their pups played with her jewels. She made herself clothes of hides and furs, but sometimes she walked the ridges with no clothes on at all. When she died, the dogs followed their natures and eventually buried her bones.

I was sorry to find Jezebel's loss of her body back in the version I was offering Ruth, but it felt necessary to the telling, and true.

Ruth had picked up a stick and was drawing circles in the dirt. When I finished, she nodded once, then jumped up as if she'd decided something. "Come on," she said, "I've got something to show you."

I wanted to write in the sun, but Ruth was rare company, so when she offered her scrawny, big-knuckled hand, I took it and let her pull me to my feet.

We walked down to the creek, talking about Miss Alice. Ruth was trying to get me to enter Miss Alice in the Moody livestock show. I would not dream of doing anything of the sort, but it was pleasant to walk with Ruth towards the cottonwoods that lined the creek and list Miss Alice's qualifications for a blue-ribbon championship: her well-attached udder and high milk production, her sweet disposition, the flat curls on her forehead and her glints of gold.

The creek was running low, so there was room to walk side by side along its sandy edge. For weeks, I had been dry with the suspicion of water in a basin or a bucket or a pump, but the sound of it gurgling and splashing against itself in the streambed soothed me as it always had. A big round rock in the distance made me blink and startle; for a moment I thought it was Martha bending to roll down her stockings and step into the creek. Ruth threw a handful of gravelly sand into the water, and said, "We're almost there, Mrs. Linger. Keep coming."

We rounded a curve that returned everything behind us to mystery once it was out of sight. I had always loved this about the creek: that it led me to fish in its shallows and absorbed me in its rocks and falls with no relation to the road or the farm or anything I had learned in the world.

Ruth whistled "Sweet Betsy from Pike," then stopped next to the thick roots of a willow exposed in the bank. "Here it is," she said. "This is my cavern."

It was a large dark hole between two roots, and as I peered into it, I remembered eyes watching as I rinsed my arms and wept after Mr. Balm had reached for me. "Can you crawl in there?" I asked. "Did you watch me?"

Ruth nodded, embarrassed. "I saw you crying down here once, but that's not why I have it. I don't use it to spy. I keep things for myself in there. Like Jezebel from the Bible in the wild dog dens. You just told me."

I didn't like the picture of Ruth curled up in this hole like a cornered fox. I put my hands on the roots. "What things?"

Ruth reached past me with both arms and stuck her head in the hole. "It gets wider," she said hollow-voiced from inside. I heard the rustling of leaves or papers, then she emerged with handfuls of pebbles that had been rounded in the creek.

"Jewels. Ammunition." She spilled the flat, smooth stones from one hand to the other, then back again. "Secrets."

She offered me a rock, and I took it, suddenly aware that I was a big-hipped farm wife with land and a garden and a cow, and she was a scrawny little girl with fast legs and rocks for secrets. I didn't want to play anymore. "Thanks for showing me, Ruth. I'd better be getting back."

I tried to hand her the rock, which was striped with veins of white and speckled black and pink and rust in turn. "Keep it," she said, and I put it in my apron pocket and headed up the bank towards the house.

I didn't go inside for my pen and writing pad, but went straight to the garden to take care of my responsibilities and weed the onions. I worked bent over with the blood running to my head as Jezebel pulsed and changed into Martha Moody standing in the council of wild dogs and leading the dance for meat.

Every now and then I looked up to watch Ruth coax Miss Alice to a stump so she could ride her. Miss Alice kept dropping her head to crop mouthfuls of grass, but she went where she was led, and stood patiently as Ruth kicked off her heavy brown shoes and clambered onto the cow's back. Ruth didn't try to get Miss Alice to go any place in particular, but wrapped her arms around her neck as they wandered from clumps of grass to the salt lick to the trough, then on to more grass. When Miss Alice stood quietly chewing her cud, Ruth stretched out on her stomach and held on with just her bare, mud-spattered legs.

I carried three buckets full of parsnips and turnips to the root cellar to sort into bins, and was coming up the earthen steps imagining Martha throwing a bundle of singing grasses on a bonfire, when I saw a group of women on horseback in the distance. There was no mistaking Theda Wilks with her fine carriage and plumed hat. I crouched and pulled the flat door closed above me. I didn't hear much while I was hiding there in the dark, but I kept myself calm by sorting parsnips and turnips by feel, setting each one softly in its bin, so they wouldn't hear me overhead. They called my name for a while, and I heard Theda telling Ruth to get off that cow, then there was a long time when all I heard was snatches of their voices and doors creaking open and closed.

I had emptied all three buckets before I heard them mount their horses and ride away. I waited a while longer, then opened the door and climbed out of the root cellar wishing that I had met them with an axe and run them off my land.

There were footprints in the garden. Someone had bit into a tomato, then left it half pink and open on the ground. Miss Alice was looking at me over the fence with interested eyes, but Ruth was nowhere to be seen.

I went to the house, and found that they had swept the floor, emptied the stove of ashes, and left me a note on the kitchen table under the clean black skillet:

> *Dear Mrs. Linger,*
> *We stopped by to offer solace in your time of trouble, but did not find you at home. We remember you in our prayers and miss you in church. Please come.*
>
> *Your sisters in Christ,*
> *The Ladies Committee*
> *P.S. We ran off a neighbor child who was harassing your livestock.*

Next to the skillet was a heaping bowl of Theda's three-bean salad.

The note haunted me for days. I knew Theda had looked down at me from her horse and spat "lunatic" in my face, but the salad was delicious and the message on the note was so mild. I liked seeing my name written in her elegant script, and I was getting used to the idea of being remembered in their prayers. The truth was that I was lonely for the sound of other voices. On Sunday, I decided to go into town.

I pulled my hair back with my best brass comb, and put on my corset. I even splashed my face with water, trying not to be uncouth. I put on a clean blouse and a dark blue serge skirt, then walked down to the edge of the road feeling timid.

I fingered my cameo brooch and steeled myself for proving to Theda Wilks that I could pass for decent as well as she could. I thought of other times I had walked into Moody. Some women from church had walked past me as if I weren't there, while others made harsh comments as I passed, sending the edges of their voices towards me sharp with disapproval. It must have taken an act of Christian charity for them to invite me back into the fold—I had to give them that.

The town was quiet when I arrived. I was late for church. The photograph of Martha still hung in the store window, and there was a big sign up at the railroad station: "YOU'VE FOUND IT! HOME OF MARTHA MOODY, BELLE OF THE WEST." I cringed with embarrassment when I read that, but a restaurant had opened on Main Street and buildings were going up. Moody was booming.

The Reverend was citing Scripture when I slipped in the door. I sat in the back next to a woman named Opal Gunn, who was holding a new baby. She smiled and nodded absently at me, as if she couldn't remember my name.

The Reverend had a head cold. His text was the Beatitudes, and he wiped his nose after each "blessed are."

Mr. Balm sat in the Moody pew at the front of the church, but Martha wasn't with him. I had hoped to be able to watch her as I had in the past: big, brisk, wearing black, filling half the pew with her flesh and God's grace. Instead, there was the back of Theda Wilks' swan neck across the aisle.

The Reverend wrapped up his reading with a wet cough, and we rose for a hymn. I heard Clara's strong alto, and found the back of her second-best dress through the crowd. Clay was stooping down to her so that they could share a hymnal. The frizzed knot of her hair caught at my heart.

It was pleasant to be among people again, lulled by the long hymn and the scent of the lilac water Opal wore, but I slipped back into the sunshine before the last amen. I had been months without talking to the people of Moody, and those few moments of listening had been enough. Besides, I could not face Clara and Theda and the others on the steps after the service, so I cut behind the station to the railroad tracks and walked out a ways to rest my mind.

I walked along the track, feeling the cold wind, and thinking that I should come into town more often, try to learn again the proper way to act. The wind was blowing strands of hair in my face, so I pulled my comb loose, and let my hair blow back. It was a bright day, with thunderheads piling themselves in the west, so that the sky seemed more blue where it showed through the gaps in the clouds. I saw a figure coming out of the prairie, skipping along one rail like a dancer. I thought it was Ruth, until I saw the gold glinting off his horn. It was John.

I stood still and watched him approach. His arms were out to keep his balance, and his white sleeves hung loose in the wind. His horn was tied to his waist with a red sash, and it bounced against his thigh.

He looked strange, but I was not afraid. He was staring at the rail beneath his feet, and I didn't think he'd seen me, until he stopped running and slid on his black shoes to the place where I was standing by the tracks.

He turned his head to look at me with his sky-blue eyes. They were sharp. "Hello."

He sounded too much like my husband. I stepped back. "John, what are you doing?"

My friends at dances used to lick their lips to signify John. Now he smiled with his lush mouth. "Ask yourself that, unnatural monster."

He didn't sound mean. He fiddled with the edge of his sash.

He's a child, I decided. "Don't call people monster, John," I said aloud, "and you shouldn't be walking on the tracks."

I reached for the white sleeve that I had starched so many times, but he skipped away from me up the rail. He turned on his toes and looked back at me. "Don't touch me. You're not my wife."

He looked so slight that I wondered why I ever let him hit my face. I held my hands in the air. "I won't, then. I'm glad to hear that I'm not your wife."

He nodded and pushed the valves of his horn. "How's Miss Alice?" John didn't milk her, but he had bought her curry comb, and used to brush her until she shone.

"You know how she is. You sneak to the barn to see her, don't you?"

He beat his fingers on the dented bell. "She always loved Sousa."

I remembered sitting at the kitchen table with John's cold supper, waiting long hours while he played in the barn with the boys. They had left circles of tobacco stains in the hay on the floor. They stopped playing if I came out, and looked at me, waiting for me to go back to the house. I grew to hate most of the hymns they knew. I sat in my old cotton wrapper, picking at John's hunk of cornbread and reading about how Ruth clave unto Naomi and said, "Intreat me not to leave thee, or to return from following after thee: for whither thou goest, I will go; and where thou lodgest, I will lodge: thy people shall be my people and thy God my God."

"You were a disappointment as a husband," I said to John.

"I was never your husband," he said flatly.

That annoyed me. I had kept his house and his company for nine years. "You didn't marry the cow." Then I heard the whistle. "John, it's the train. Get off the track."

He turned back and forth on his toes, ignoring me. I saw the dark shape of the train on the far edge of my sight. I tried to grab his sleeve to pull him from the track, and he feinted a kick at me. I ducked his foot. "You're so theatrical. Let the train hit you, then." I turned my back.

The earth started to shake, as it always did when the train came. I took a step. When I heard the whistle again, a hard-won second sense made me crouch to the ground. John's body came flying over my head. The train rushed past. I didn't know if John was alive or dead until I knelt beside him and saw him grin. He still smelled like French soap. "I jumped."

I stood up, torn between a desire to kick gravel in his face and the impulse to fetch him water. "How could you be so stupid?"

"I want to talk to you."

His horn had come untied and was lying some distance away in the deep grass. I walked over and picked it up. "The last time we spoke, you attacked me. The sheriff says you've forgotten all that."

He sat up and wiped his mouth with his hand. "I remember."

I handed him his horn. "I would have let the train hit you."

John hugged his instrument and nodded. "Nothing you could do."

I sat down on the grass, out of his arms' reach, and crossed my arms. "You could talk without feigning suicide or practically knocking me to the ground. What is it you have to tell me? I don't have anything to do with you."

He kept looking at his horn. "Amanda, do you have unnatural passions?"

I had to laugh. He looked so earnest and tragic, with his gaunt face and shining hair, mud on his cheek and a rip in his linen shirt. He had read my stories about Martha and come after me in a fury. This question did not deserve an answer. "I don't know what you mean."

John took offense. "You must tell me what is amusing you."

In the distance I could hear the voices of people getting off the train at Moody station. Men and women greeted each other, talking loudly. If I listened hard I could recognize most of the voices, but, as it was, I let their talk slide off me like a bird song that I recognized, but couldn't name.

I pulled out a handful of red clover and threw it at John. One round purple flower slid into the bell of his horn. "It's too late in our marriage for me to start talking about my passions with you, John."

John turned red and brushed the clover from his shirt. His mouth tightened, and I put my hand on a rock. Then he looked down and shook the flower from his horn into his palm. He popped it into his mouth, and we had a moment of grace.

"Red clover soothes the nerves," he said, chewing.

We both laughed, and I let go of the rock. "I'm so sorry," said John, "for being rough."

I said nothing. He stood up then. He didn't deserve the sun on his bright hair, but I saw him spark. He tied his horn around his waist again. "I'll go."

I nodded. As I watched him walk towards Moody, he dulled and looked blurry, as if he had stretched to a thin spot, distorted, and was about to break. He passed the station. I looked away.

Eleven

The fall passed in a flood of tomatoes, squash and beans. I put up enough vegetables to last a big family the winter, so I wouldn't run low come spring.

I tried to hire Ruth to help me when my canning was at its height, but she chewed her hair and said, "No kitchen work." She helped dig the potatoes and gather the yellow squash before it was overripe, but she came and went as she pleased, and left the full bushel baskets outside the door.

The cold came. I started lighting the fire at night because I couldn't stand the cold sheets. I strung a rope line between the house and the barn so I wouldn't have to worry about getting lost and freezing on the way to feed Miss Alice when the snows came. They did come, blown into hard heaps against the house.

I baked, wrote, read the Bible, dug out. Some days the sun would hit the snow so that it flooded my eyes with colors, and I lost the shapes of things. I found a pair of John's skis in the barn. They were too long for me, but I took a few turns around the pasture, falling when I picked up speed.

Martha's adventures got weirder. She dug herself into the ground with her bare hands chasing a rabbit for supper, and ended up in a silver cavern, where the walls and floors were polished slick. She followed a green river to get back to surface rocks and dirt. Another time she was dragged a hundred miles behind a wild horse, and dug a canyon with her heels. One story that Frank sent back as too lurid had Martha leading the town in battle against an aging band of ex-Confederate soldiers. The one-eyed leader chopped off Martha's right breast before she shot him, so forever after she had a flat place on her chest to steady her rifle, which improved her aim.

Frank penciled in a note across the top of that story. "Not so much agony, Mrs. Linger. We love Martha Moody. Don't you?"

I never answered. My mind had chased itself in circles over that question, but it wasn't his business. Martha kept her breast. I pictured Frank sitting in an office in Chicago in a striped shirt, smoking a cigar and writing me checks. That was all I wanted from him.

I took pride in how I thrived in the long silence of those days, but every time I baked a loaf of bread that came out heavy, I blamed Martha's pressure in the house. She had never been there in body; she had left me flat, cold, and aching, but I tasted her in loaves and sweets. Despite the snatches of music, John had no such ghost.

Sometimes I barely spoke to Ruth after she had made it through snow drifts into Moody to buy me salt and flour, for fear I'd ask too much about Martha.

I was free as a woman could hope to be, but, in the words of the Scripture, my bones were burned. I had Martha dive into lava. Her dress scorched off, but she had rubbed the angel-cow's butter over her skin, where it glistened and protected her from burns. Martha climbed unscathed onto the rim of the volcano, and dressed herself in a cloud of maidenly steam that allowed Frank to run the story in all its heat.

One morning after milking Miss Alice and baking two loaves of pumpkin bread, I wrapped one in a tea cloth and walked through the field to Clara's. There was no path, so I sank in snow over my boots, and my stockings were soaked. My teeth were chattering when I knocked on her back door. She opened the door in a thick, quilted gown with a ruffle of muslin and ribbons and lace. She looked as perishable as red-leaf lettuce, but she stepped out into snow past her ankles and threw her arms around me as far as they would go. I could barely feel her hug through my cloak, but I felt the warmth as she drew me into the room. Clara took my cloak and hung it next to the stove. It hissed and dripped over the big pot of water that sat next to the fire to give moisture to the dry coal heat. She pulled my head down and gave me a kiss on the mouth. "I'm so glad you've come, Amanda. I've missed you." I handed her my loaf. I didn't know what to say. Clara set the pumpkin bread on the table, put the kettle on. "Take off your boots. I'll get dry stockings." She kicked off her soaked slippers and hurried out of the room. I sat at Clara's table and took my boots off. The air smelled as if Clara had been cooking with sage. I leaned my elbows on the table, and breathed her back in as a friend. She returned to the kitchen wearing dry wool stockings and carrying a pair of Clay's thick socks for me. "I knew mine would never fit," she said, then she knelt with a towel to rub my feet. I put my hand on her thin shoulder with its padded silk. "Stop, Clara. I can do that."

She looked up at me. "But they're blue with cold."

I couldn't say, Martha's hands on my ankles, warm water, soap, Holy Jesus. "Sit down and talk with me. Quit fussing."

She tucked the towel around my feet, and pulled her chair close to mine. She cut a thick slice of pumpkin bread and handed it to me. "Amanda, it's been too long."

I took the slice, broke it, and gave her back half. "I brought it for you. Eat with me."

It was so easy. We drank tea, and talked about the weather, Theda Wilks' spat with the Reverend, Clay's angina. Clara spread another slice with butter, saying, "I've been aching for some of Miss Alice's good cream."

It was almost as if she were courting me. She kept touching my hand and refilling my tea cup. She complimented my hair, which was curling in the steam of the kitchen, and said nothing about my man's shirt. She looked beautiful to me, too, her small shoulders in her soft robe, the way she leaned intently over the table to tell me how the postmaster had gone to Chicago to join the circus as the tattooed man. "I never even knew he'd been at sea."

She brushed the crumbs from her ruffle, then said, "I've seen *True Western Tales*. I've bought every one."

I felt an edge of the old anger, but sipped my tea and let it pass. "He pays me well."

Clara poured me more, rested her fingers on my wrist. "Do you see Martha?"

I thought I would slam the cup down, or hiss in her eager, pink face. I thought I could not talk of Martha with Clara, who knew everyone's secret hearts, and diagrammed many of them for the public view. But I was warm and lulled and lonely, and I told her the truth.

Not the bare truth; I lingered. I went back to what I'd thought of Martha before we'd ever touched.

"Martha has always had power."

"Of course," said Clara, "the store."

"She supplies the candies, the tobacco, the buckets, dried apples, everything. Her name is the name of the town. Men address themselves to her, women defer. The gossip about her failed marriage was that her husband was afraid of her."

Clara was playing with the butter, drawing circles on it with her knife. "He wanted to go all the way to California. She defied him, and he was so weak as to leave her to build her house here and sell some of his goods." Her voice was low, incantatory. She was reciting lore. "The marriage is not mentioned often."

I fell into the rhythm. "No, people owe her money. She sits at the front pew in church. Everybody knows she has outbursts. Once or twice a year, after months of mumbling, Martha belts out, 'Just a closer walk with thee . . .'"

Clara cut a sliver of butter, smeared it across her saucer. "She veers from the melody, but she can project. She's stopped coming on Sundays. The stories are making her famous. She gets thronged."

I blew on my tea. "She must hate that. Is she still rumored to be a secret drinker?"

Clara shook her head. "No, open. Martha never took the temperance pledge. You know she drank *something* from a goblet on the boardwalk the day Mrs. Nation came to town."

My face was hot. I hugged myself. "Yes. She had nothing on her conscience that morning. I took a bottle of wine from the saloon."

"I remember. I saw you."

"I was looking for protection when I ran up her back alley with the bottle under my cloak and spirits soaking my shoes. I found lightning on my body as she moved her hands over my feet. She pushed herself across me with a weight that took my breath. I rocked her sex on my breast, and her hair fell on my legs like wonder." I could barely breathe as I spoke.

Clara touched my fingers. "Wasn't it strange? Weren't you surprised?"

She had read the stories. She was the only one I could speak to, and I hadn't spoken at all for so long. "No. I was ready. I was glad."

Clara was silent. She kept her hand stretched across the table so that the tips of her fingers touched mine on the cup. I took a great breath, then fell again to talking. "When her father came, I lost her. I lost her when my husband forced me to the public road. I don't know which cut her from me. It wasn't that she'd had her fill of me. It was her childhood up to haunt her or her father's disapproval or the loss of respect and what that meant to her livelihood at the store. It was something to be understood. I had to understand.

"She looked at me with visible pain. That much was visible: pain and desire. I wanted her to tell me. I wanted words, or clear signs from her body. Sex with her had wrenched me into light. She leaned against me every time we saw each other, but then she drew away.

"We had the language of the body. For me, for a time, that was enough. I had never spoken freely, never in my life. But when touch was blocked, light was forced into my throat. I wanted talk. I wanted to know what it was she was leaving me for. If the light couldn't soothe itself against Martha, it had to have someplace to go.

"For me it was words, talking, talking, talking. I couldn't speak to Martha, so I wrote. I write. Sometimes I am explicit, but it is incomplete without her voice. The tales make her magic, lift her into air, make buildings fall away around her. It's part truth, part code, part wish."

I looked at Clara. Her face was wet with kitchen steam. "It was a violation when you found them, but it was also a relief."

Then I stopped. I was sweating from the coal heat and melted snow, shocked to find that I had a passion for exposure and a taste for talk as strong as Clara's, but more reckless, since I was talking about my own love and my heart.

Clara lifted her small fingers and pressed them into the butter. They left prints. "I'm sorry, Amanda."

She let me wash the cups and saucers while she wiped the table and tidied up. We hugged hard when I left. There was nothing more to say that made sense.

I still heard horn music in the barn at night. John no longer scared me, but I didn't seek him out. There was nothing he could help me with, and it felt dangerous to try to help him.

I heard him late one night when the snow was whipping in circles outside my window. It was not a night for walking, so I knew he must be in the barn. I listened for a while as the music broke off in scraps and drifted to the house, the only sounds against the roaring of the wind.

I was awake after the playing stopped. I had heated stones on the stove and warmed my sheets with them, and I had already crawled under the covers and began to undress there, when I sat bolt upright and let the quilts fall down around me. I didn't want the man to freeze to death, so I got out of bed and dressed to go outdoors.

I found the rope that marked the way to the barn, and slid my hand along it. It was slick and icy. I gripped as tightly as I could. The light from the house was blotted out in the blowing snow. I carried a lantern, but its flickering light was of little use. When I lost my footing and fell, it went out on its side in a drift.

I let go of the rope as I fell, afraid the line would snap, but I could see it swinging in the air, and I grabbed it from flat on my back. Then I got up slowly, and started again for the barn. I left the lantern where it lay, and held onto the rope with both hands.

I walked into the side of the barn with a small sliding step, then felt my way along splintery boards to the door.

A cloud of snow and wind followed me into the barn before I got the door latched behind me. It was dry and still inside, but very cold. I could hear Miss Alice's slow breathing. I shook the snow off my cape. As my eyes adjusted to the darkness, I saw something moving next to Miss Alice in her stall.

I walked over to find John sitting on a mound of hay and staring about him in a half dream that I recognized from years of sharing a bed. "It's all right, John," I said, softly. "I brought you something warm."

Under my cloak, I had tied two blankets that had come dry through the snow. I untied them and spread them over him, and he sank down in the hay again without a word. He nestled close to Miss Alice. Her body rose and fell with her breath, which clouded in the cold air.

I pulled the food I had brought him out of my pockets: bread, cheese, a crock of beans. He could milk Miss Alice in the morning. I looked at the lines their bodies made sleeping close for comfort and warmth, and remembered his thin arm reaching over my belly to hold me as we drifted in our bed. Miss Alice worked as well for him as I had for a companion in the night. That was not to say she was enough, or made him happy.

John and I had tried to be simple with each other, breaking our inner lives down to what we needed for survival. I wanted him to live through this blizzard night, but I didn't want him sleeping in the barn. It was his as much as mine, but as I listened to the rustling rats, Miss Alice breathing, and the wind, I thought he needed other, human pleasure in his life.

That was my night of weakness, when I forgot my anger and wanted for John everything I wanted for myself, and had to go out through the blizzard to give him all that I could: two blankets, a small mound of food.

I tucked the blanket over his feet, spread more hay around Miss Alice, then fastened my cloak to make my way back to the house through the snow.

The winter passed in this way. My isolation was much eased after I started speaking with Clara again. She and Clay had me over to dinner, and Clara stopped by often, bringing me sourdough starter, or a magazine, or news from town. She offered to do my shopping for me, but I liked to see Ruth coming across the field knocking snow caps off the fence posts with a stick. Once Clara was eating dried apple fritters in my kitchen when Ruth tromped to the back door with my supplies.

I took the bags from her. "Come in, Ruth. Have a roll. Do you know Mrs. Spencer?"

Ruth hung back by the door, and bobbed a curtsy to Clara, pulling her skirt from under her coat on both sides. My mouth dropped open. She had never been that formal with me, and looked odd dipping her purple skirt up over her big boots.

Clara bowed her head to her lace collar. "Nice to meet you, Ruth. I know your mother from church."

When Ruth left with two apple fritters in her pocket, Clara said, "That's a wild girl. She broke Henry Pickney's finger in a fight after school."

I shrugged. "She loves Miss Alice."

Clara raised one eyebrow. "I swear, that cow has more admirers—you would think she could rise and fly." She gave me three quick winks. I stuck out my tongue. We laughed.

I started tomato seedlings inside while there was still snow on the ground. I set them at the window in the light and next to the stove at dark. They were green company.

Sometimes I read aloud to them from the Bible at night: "And when the day of Pentecost was fully come, they were all with one accord in one place. And suddenly there came a sound from heaven as of a rushing mighty wind, and it filled all the house where they were sitting. And there appeared unto them cloven tongues like as of fire, and it sat upon each of them. And they were all filled with the Holy Ghost, and began to speak with other tongues, as the Spirit gave them utterance."

I looked at the tomato plants, but they showed no inclination to speak. I kept after the Bible because it lit me up inside like nothing else. My eyes slid over the moral instruction, and locked into the power of the words. "My bones are pierced in me in the night season: and my sinews take no rest."

The plants stretched. Their stems began to bristle, and their leaves gave off a biting tomato smell. The days passed.

I wrote a story without Martha. Some children bury their father in the garden up to his neck, and feed him dirt until he chokes to death. His ghost comes up with lettuces. The children eat salad that makes them bitter beyond belief, and they live in hatred together to a ripe age.

It was an awful story. I put it in a drawer under some of John's old socks.

Then I wrote another without Martha: a fat woman joins the circus and masters the trapeze. She performs in yellow tights and a midlength blue shirt that falls over her head to make her look like a flower, her belly the yellow center, when she does a back bend on the platform high above the crowd. She is a steady partner for the somersaults of the other artists. She drops from the trapeze to catch them, holding on to the apparatus with her thick, pliant legs. She leaps from one swing to another, and does a split in midair. The crowd throws her flowers, which she catches in her teeth.

She engages in a duel of wills with the ringmaster, who grows jealous of her fame, and wants to switch her to an elephant act. Carmelita resists him, but she is shaken by his plotting. One night she kisses her old clown father before she climbs to the post to do a triple twist and plummets to her death. The ringmaster realizes that he always loved her, and the big top is shrouded in black every night for the rest of his lifetime to commemorate her plunge.

I shipped that one off to Frank. He wrote back to say that it didn't work for *True Western Tales,* but he thought he could place it in one of his other rags. He asked me what name he should use.

I stuffed a turkey with cornbread and biscuits while I searched my heart for the answer. I consulted Clara and Miss Alice, then I wrote him to say that my name was "Virginia Delaflor."

It was almost Amanda Linger, but I hadn't thrown respectability to the winds, not yet.

I was ready for the thaw when it came. I put the tomatoes in the ground when it was still cold mud because they were going to stem in their flats.

I put up screens and left my doors and windows open all day. I lit citronella candles and moved the heating bricks out of my bed. I got Ruth to help me clean the flue.

Miss Alice left hunks of gold-brown hair on the doorposts of the barn where she leaned to scratch her sides. Her udders hung so low they almost dragged the ground, so I watched her teats for dirt and cuts when I milked. Her milk was drying up some, too.

I blamed the change in the seasons. I thought of borrowing Clay's bull to breed her, but I was in no rush. I took walks with her around the pasture, although it was more mud than grass at that time of year. I didn't use a lead. Miss Alice came when I called her name.

I was getting bigger. John's shirts began to gap at the lower buttons over my belly, so I pulled old blouses from the bureau drawers, and found they no longer fit. My skirts were more accommodating. I just let them out at the waist, and they fell over my fuller hips with as much practicality and grace as they ever had. John's old loose jacket still fit, but I let out or made over all of my dresses, and put his shirts away. It seemed wasteful to use them for rags.

My clothes had become a calendar. I was making my peace with water, and found the patience to set the washpot over the fire for laundry every two weeks or so. When every skirt I had was crusted at the hem with barn-yard mud, I knew that the laundry period had passed, but the larger cycles interested me more. As I cut the stitches that had limited the old waistbands, I grieved for my previous dimensions, so thoroughly charted by Clara's tape measure and written down in her pattern book, but this was a time of growth.

Now when I went into Moody, I dressed much as I had when I was living as John's wife, but the women still kept their distance. There was a new ice cream parlor in town, and a place that sold books. Posters of the *True Western Tales* Martha Moody and the real Martha tricked up to look like the illustration were hung in store windows and plastered to the sides of buildings, as if she were a circus that never left town. I averted my eyes, but one afternoon I walked the back alley from behind the saloon to Martha's fence, and stood at her gate looking over her garden and wishing that the sound of her voice would float to me out the kitchen door. I stood there all through the lunch hour, but I never heard so much as the clatter of a dish.

I filled a bowl with water and washed the dust of the road from my feet when I got home.

That night I had Martha over me like a cloud of smoke. She rained lust like God rained flesh on the people in the wilderness. He pelted them with the bodies of animals when they prayed for meat. They had angel food, manna, but that wasn't enough.

Martha was mostly alone in the stories now, or in the company of animals. I wrote her among creatures I had never seen, just to imagine how she looked against the shaggy pelt of a great bear, or with her hair tangled in a mountain lion's teeth.

The closest I came to her in real life was the soft sack of flour Ruth brought me from the store.

Twelve

One morning when I went out to milk her, Miss Alice was standing very still, chewing her cud, as if lost in thought. I gave her a swat on the rump to get her to go to her stall for milking, and she moved with a jerk that was nothing like her usual swaying walk. I sat down on the stool, and patted her flank. Miss Alice had a habit of looking over her shoulder at me at least once while I milked her, but this morning she stared straight ahead. The bucket was less than a quarter full when I gave up.

Ruth propped open the barn door, letting in cool, grey light. She looked at me sitting on the stool with my hands in my lap, the bucket with its puddle of milk between my legs. "Is that all?" she asked me, then, without waiting for an answer, she wrapped her arm around the cow's neck and was crooning in her ear. "Is that all, Alice, Miss Alice Alice? Is that all the milk from a fine milker this morning?"

The cow didn't move. She just chewed her cud.

"What's wrong with her?" Ruth looked at me, twisting her wild hair.

"I'm not sure. She's been off her feed. I'll try giving her some oats this morning." Ruth leaned against Miss Alice, rubbing her head on the cow's hide. "I won't ride her today."

I didn't like to see Ruth bending every which way, and Miss Alice standing so stiff, just chewing. "I'll get my list," I said. "You go on to the store."

After Ruth left, I went back to the barn and felt Miss Alice's muzzle. It was dry. She had a fever. I got a bucket of fresh water and set it near her head so she could easily drink, then I filled another bucket and splashed it over her, thinking to cool her off. Miss Alice snorted when I poured the water, and I came around to scratch under her jaw. I wanted to talk to her like I usually would, but I couldn't think of anything to say, so I just hummed. "Mmmmmm, mmmm. Miss Alice."

She blinked, and I saw that her eyes were sunken. "Mmmmmmm, mmmmmmm, Miss Alice. Mmmmmm, mmmmmm, mmmmmm."

I offered her some oats, and she ate a little from my hand. Her lips felt stiff. I lifted the bucket to give her water, but she wouldn't bend her head. I cupped my palms together and held water to her mouth. She didn't drink.

I opened my hands and let the water spill against my skirt. My own eyes felt hot and burning, as if Miss Alice had my body under her hide. I bent over and stretched both arms around her, checking for bloat. I had my face against her shoulder, and I was shaking, when someone touched my hip.

I jerked my head. It was Ruth. "I could go for the blacksmith," she said. "If you want I could go ask him what to do."

The town blacksmith knew animals as well as he knew iron, and he was called in times of sickness to barns for miles around.

I stood up, keeping one hand on Miss Alice's back. My dress was wet where I had spilled. "Tell him she's still chewing cud, but her nose is dry and her eyes are sunken and she won't drink."

Ruth took off again, running.

I kept offering oats and water to Miss Alice, but she wouldn't take any more. I tried hay and grass and molasses, but she just stared straight ahead. I combed her all over. Her hair felt dry. Her jaw worked slowly, but the rest of her never moved.

She felt so hot. I wanted her to drink. I held up the bucket with the dribble of her own milk in it, and I thought I saw her stretch her neck. I scooped up the milk in my hands, and held it out to her. She made no move to drink.

I thought I was calmly trying to help a farm animal, like anyone would do. I thought it made sense that she might drink her own milk when she would not take water or food.

When she wouldn't drink, I splattered the milk back into the bucket, absently wiping my hands on my skirt. Then I went out to the shady side of the barn where I had set yesterday's milking in covered pans on a shelf for the cream to rise.

I took the copper bowl off the shelf and skimmed the cream from the pans with a fork. I walked with the bowl full of cream and the fork back into the barn to sit with Miss Alice.

She was almost motionless, chewing cud. I sat down on the stool next to her, and started to whip the cream.

I beat it with the fork, tilting the bowl. The fork clanged against the sides. My head hurt. A froth built on the cream. I kept beating. It didn't get thicker. I dipped my finger in it. The froth clung to my finger, and I thought, "Milk doesn't cling. It must be changing."

My thoughts were that slow. Miss Alice stood and chewed. I felt like I had been up all night crying. My head forced itself on me as a physical presence: it hurt, it was heavy, and it held my few thoughts like the bowl held the cream. A fly circled, and I brushed it away. Miss Alice's sides made small movements as she breathed.

The froth stiffened. I turned the fork, folding in air. I watched Miss Alice chew. I was stuck in the same motions over and over: whip the cream, watch Miss Alice, whip. An image floated into my head of Martha raising her black skirt to let me run my hands over her thighs. I closed my eyes to let it pass, and opened my eyes to Miss Alice chewing her cud.

I got tired. My arm was sore, moving mechanically through the froth. It wouldn't change. It was only froth. I watched her sides for the faint rise of breath. I tried to think of why I was handling food in the barn, but my mind couldn't find an edge to catch on, and kept slopping over the rim of the bowl. I was very scared. Miss Alice chewed her cud. The froth suddenly smoothed into cream again, but thick. It became a bowlful of clouds, but I kept whipping past the point where it was light and sweet. I could hear the soft rustle of rats in the loft. I leaned over and dipped my soft chins in the bowl, then wiped my face with the side of my finger. I licked the finger; the cream melted as soon as my tongue found it. I barely had to swallow: it dribbled down my throat like water, only rich.

"I'm crazy," I thought as I got up to offer some cream to Miss Alice. I dipped my finger in the bowl, then ran it along her gums. She opened her mouth, and I put my dripping finger on her tongue, with the damp bits of old chewed grass. Her mouth smelled like beer, but I got a little cream to dribble into her throat before she clamped her jaw shut.

She wouldn't open again, so I went back to beating. My fingers were stiff, so I switched hands. The cream changed quickly. It had already lost its fluff and sheen, and a watery liquid was pooling at the edges of the bowl. The clouds were breaking down into lumps, so I stopped stirring and gathered them into a ball with my hands. I squeezed and smoothed it. It was butter. I was offering buttered oats to Miss Alice when Ruth and the blacksmith came.

He felt her muzzle and pulled down the skin around her eyes. He measured her girth. He ran his hands up and down her sides. "She take any water or food?"

I wiped my hands on my skirt. "A little bit of oats this morning."

He walked to his horse and pulled a piece of rubber hosing from his saddle bag. "She's dried out. Who knows why. Only thing I know to do is to force water down her throat, but if she gets it in her lungs, she could drown. Sometimes they do."

I let him do it. I helped him. He got her mouth open, I stuck the tube to the back of her throat, and we funneled water in. Green water spilled from the sides of her mouth, and her eyes went wild, but she must have swallowed, because she was breathing when he pulled the hose out.

I brought the blacksmith a towel. "If she goes down on her side, turn her from hip to hip if you can. Stops gas from building up inside her." Then he wished me luck and left.

Ruth was whispering in Miss Alice's ear. I stood beside her. "Come on, angel cow," she said. "Come on, Azreal."

Miss Alice was hiccuping a little, and breathing ragged. She wasn't chewing cud anymore.

I brought Ruth a chair from the kitchen, and we sat silently watching the cow's sides rise and fall.

When it happened, there was no one with me. Ruth had to go home at dusk. She cried, but I thought of her mother, and made her go. I hugged her skinny shoulders.

Miss Alice was trying to wait for John, I thought, but he didn't come. Her breathing was uneven for hours. When she dropped to her side, I tried to turn her, but she was too heavy for me to move. She felt cooler, but she was blowing hard through her nostrils. I held her head in my lap with its stains of dried milk and butter grease. She looked at me once. Then she died.

When John slipped in the door very late carrying his horn, he found me sitting by her body on the ground. It must have been a shock of grief for him, farmer though he was, but he did careful, necessary things.

I saw his face was wet when he helped me to my feet. He spread a blanket on the hay. He closed her eyes and pulled a blanket over Miss Alice, then he helped me loosen my hair and lie down. He stretched out between Miss Alice's body and me, and gently stroked my hair. I stared stiffly at the rafters for a long, long time; then, as bodies will, mine slept.

In the morning, John walked over to the Spencers' house and asked for Clay's help and his cart. Clay was kind and asked no questions about John's return. He brought his hired boy, and they took Miss Alice from the barn in the mule-drawn cart.

I didn't go with them to dig the hole. Clara came to help me wash the hay from my hair. She said, "I know you loved her," as if Miss Alice were my child, and I burst into tears in her arms.

———

Ruth didn't come back for a week. I sat at the kitchen table and worried about her. She must have seen the death of animals before, but not one like Miss Alice, whose secret name she knew.

I tried to get interested in working in the garden. I had flats of seedlings that were ready to go into the ground, but I just set them outside where I wouldn't have to look at their crowded, skinny green tops. Eventually John turned over the topsoil in a couple beds, and planted everything that I had started.

As the weather warmed, John was living openly in the barn. He hadn't asked me, but just started wandering out to use the pump to douse his face in the mornings. I didn't mind. It was odd to see fastidious John wash in cold water and wear old blue workclothes to spare his linen the hay and dirt, but I didn't offer to heat his water or wash his clothes. I did take his stack of shirts from the drawer and leave them on a bale of hay for him to find. He didn't seem dangerous to me, even when he started doing work around the place, but I stayed inside, away from him and the glare of the days.

I made a big pot of baked beans, and got up to stir it now and again as the beans softened and sweetened and stuck to the bottom of the pot. Mostly I sat at the kitchen table, sorted through my old papers, and wrote. I had hand-copied every story I'd sent to Frank; now I found every one that mentioned Azreal and made a separate stack of them, with the sugar bowl as a paperweight to keep them from blowing around. I didn't read through them again; I just looked for her name, then set the pages aside.

Clara brought me a German chocolate cake, her mother's recipe that she made for holidays and wakes. I was touched, and offered her a bowl of the beans.

Clara sat with the warm bowl in her hands for a moment before I realized that she had no place to set it on the table. I moved the Azreal stories, and the stacks of old Martha stories, new Martha stories, stories without Martha, scraps and notes and ideas.

"I've never seen all this paper out in the light of day before." Clara took a spoonful of beans, and smacked her lips over its seasoned molasses taste.

"No, you managed to find it under a mattress." I didn't intend to sound bitter, but I didn't know how to talk about my work.

Clara put down her spoon. "Amanda, are you holding a grudge?"

I shook my head and ate my beans, so I could get to the cake and exclaim. I did appreciate Clara, but it was an edgy time.

Clara ran her finger through some icing stuck to the cake plate, and licked it. "I saw John hauling manure on my way in. Where's he sleeping?"

I looked at her face and answered her straight. "In the barn. He rinses his head every morning in the pump."

She laughed, and we relaxed. I pushed my bowl aside and picked up the knife. "Let's have some cake."

My mouthful of chocolate reminded me that I was mourning. I swallowed it slowly, then said, "It's strange to miss a cow so much, but Miss Alice was a solid part of my days."

Clara nodded. "People get attached. Clay loves those hounds of his, and cried like a baby when Sissy ripped her belly open on barbed wire, and he had to put her down."

It didn't help to eat cake and hear what anybody else had loved, but Clara was offering comfort, and I took what she offered out of tender feeling for her.

When Ruth finally came, John had gone to town. I didn't know what his errands were, but I had seen him heading off down the road in his coat and white shirt. She didn't appear with the dawn, as was her habit, but came in late morning carrying a sack of oats. My chest tightened when I saw her. She had both of her skinny arms wrapped around the burlap, and she had to keep shifting it from hip to hip and setting it down on the road.

"Good law," I thought, "she wants to feed Miss Alice." I wiped my hands on my apron and hurried out, calling, "Ruth, I've been worried about you."

She saw me coming, and waited with the sack of oats slumped at her feet. "Will you help me carry this?"

I picked up one corner of the sack and she took hold of the other, but I didn't want to walk to the barn. I had to tell her. "You know we lost Miss Alice."

She nodded. "I heard Clay Spencer talking at the store."

I wanted to ask who he was talking to and who else had heard, but Ruth started walking, so I had to ask where she wanted to go. The girl squinted out across the pasture. "To the grave."

I didn't ask any more questions, although I hadn't seen the grave myself, if you could call bare earth turned over a cow a grave. But we struck out in the direction that I'd seen the men wheel the cart, and soon enough we found the clearing in the grass, and the fresh-dug place.

Ruth took the bag from me, and tried to sling it over her shoulder, but she couldn't lift it higher than her waist. She dragged it the last few feet over the grass, then stopped, breathing hard. "I wanted to bring her something, just to mark her being gone."

I couldn't believe she'd managed to carry that bag all the way from town or her daddy's barn. I looked at her. "Ruth, where'd you get that feed?"

She sat down on the ground next to the sack on the edge of the grave. "You've been paying me, haven't you?"

I touched her hair. Someone had brushed the snarls out. Ruth must have spent everything she'd saved.

Ruth looked at me. "We need to have a service. What should we do?"

I squatted down next to her with one hand on her shoulder and one hand on the bag of grain. I couldn't think of any good Bible words for Miss Alice. Ruth and I thought for a while, then we talked a little, and decided to scatter the oats on the turned dirt.

"That will mark the place," I said. "Birds and critters will eat the oats, but some might grow."

Ruth had a jacknife tied around her neck, so she slit the bag. I lifted it to pour, and Ruth held her hands under its mouth to catch the stream of oats and sling them across the dirt. Dust rose from the oats and from the ground. They rustled as they splashed from the bag. Ruth was careful to smooth out mounds with her palms, until the brown dirt was covered with gold. I began to tell a story as we emptied the bag.

> Azreal walked the main street of Moody with her wings crossed flat on her back—hide side up, not feather side up—so for all anyone could see, she was a cow. She dogged a man's steps, so it looked to others as if he were leading her through town. He didn't turn to look at her. He was not a curious man.

They came to the front of Moody's Store, but she stopped when he went in. She walked around back to the alley, then jumped the fence into Martha's yard. She browsed in the garden a while, sidestepping the strawberries, although she left hoofprints in the lettuce bed and ate some Brussels sprouts.

When Martha came out back to water, she couldn't believe her eyes. "Azreal. What are you doing? Get out of that garden right now."

Azreal lazily opened her wings and lifted herself out of the vegetables with two great flaps. She landed next to Martha, and said, "I've always wanted to do that."

Martha snorted. "You don't need to raid the garden. You've got milk and honey any time you want."

Azreal moved her head, and the gold lining of her dark eyes caught the sun. "Martha, you're a powerful smart woman, but there's plenty you don't know."

This was the last time Martha saw Azreal, and I told Ruth what they did and what they said, but the story left me as I spoke it. I never wrote it down. Ruth listened carefully, and nodded when I stopped. She ran her hand one more time over the oats.

"Ruth, how did you know Miss Alice was Azreal?"

She looked at me. "I could see the gold in her hide. I wasn't sure. You wrote those stories."

I nodded.

"I won't tell."

I nodded again.

Ruth wrote her name with her finger in the grain, then smoothed it over and wrote, "Miss Alice."

We sat a while longer in silence, then we left. Before we had gone a hundred yards, I looked back over my shoulder and saw a bird swoop at the grain. Within a week, all of the oats were gone.

Thirteen

One morning at milking time I walked to the barn. The smell made me want to weep—hay and dry manure. John was sitting on the old stool that he had made for me, scribbling on the back of an envelope against a board on his knee. He looked up when I came in, and let his hands fall over his paper. "Morning, Amanda."

"Morning, John." He'd been doing a lot of work around the place, and we nodded when we saw each other in the course of the day, but this was the first time that I had sought him out. He looked nervous, so I took a deep breath, and said, "I want to give the place back to you. You can have it."

John closed his blue eyes for a minute, and I saw lines in his face that I'd never known as his wife. Then he opened them, and said, "What about you?"

"I have my own means of support."

John nodded slowly. He knew about the stories. I looked at him sitting on the low stool in the half dark, and I wanted to ask him if he had really lost his senses, or if that had just been an act for the sheriff after his fit of rage. The question was forming in my mouth, when I caught it for the idle curiosity it was—I didn't hate him, and I didn't want to be near him, whatever the answer. So I asked instead, "What are you writing there?"

"Writing? Oh, this. I was just doodling." He uncovered his envelope and stood up to show it to me. It was a rough sketch of the interior of the barn, with keyhole feeders and several small pens. John looked at the ground. "I've been talking to a man about goats. He says Toggenbergs give the best milk."

I knew we were done. I handed the sketch back to him, and said, "I'll move out of the house as soon as I find a place in town."

John didn't step towards me, but he reached out his hand. "Amanda, are you sure?"

I shrugged. I didn't want him to touch me. "This place was yours when I married you, John. All I brought with me was a hot dancing crush." I didn't want to reckon my years of work. I wanted to take my way out and run.

He put his hand in his pocket. We looked at each other a minute, then we both started to laugh. He was still shivering, red-faced and silly, when I turned and walked out of the barn.

I got a room at a boarding house in Moody. It wasn't Mrs. Luz's place—she had died years ago, worn out. The landlady was Mrs. Colt. She looked very young to me, with her hair piled high and falling in her face. She was always shining with heat from the kitchen when she brought in the fried chicken with gravy for dinner. At first I wanted to jump up and help her with the platters, but I held on to the edge of my chair as if my life depended on it. I couldn't let myself serve the table. The lure of the familiar was too strong.

The other boarders were mostly new to Moody, looking for jobs in the town's new prosperity. I was wearing tidy clothing and being careful about my hair to buy neutrality on the street and at the boarding house table. I ate slowly and said little more than, "Pass the butter." I spent a lot of time in my room. It was odd to have to hear the sounds of other people's lives: mumbling and footsteps and water and sometimes groans in the night.

I had brought some of last year's preserves with me, so sometimes I would open a jar of green tomato relish in my room and think about digging in the garden. I missed baking, too. I missed Miss Alice. I thought of Martha, but I didn't try to see her. Some nights I would slide my nightgown up around my neck and rub my hands over my belly and my breasts and the fat tops of my legs. It was soothing, but insufficient.

I had a table by the window. I wrote solid mornings. At first it was shocking to wake up without anything living to tend to besides myself. I kicked off the sheets, threw on my old wrapper, sat by the window and wrote until I heard the dinner bell.

In the evenings, when I was tired, I sat down with my stories and copied them all again. I didn't change anything. I just followed the old words with my fountain pen, and let my mind rest.

One morning after breakfast, I walked down to the post office and mailed everything I'd ever written to Martha. I didn't enclose a note, but I printed the return address large and clear on the outside of the package. I left my name off, though. Martha would know from the stories, but I didn't want to tempt her father to open the package before it reached her.

I didn't really expect that she would show up at my door. I just thought she had a right to see.

———

I edged into the life of the town as summer came on. Clara brought me to church once, and I sat through the whole service. Theda closed her eyes hard enough to be squinting during the recessional, so I thought she might be offering one of her special prayers for me. The ladies looked me over on the steps afterwards, and I got cordial nods. Clara's silk rustled beside me as she leaned forward to kiss every single one of them on the mouth.

She was forever talking about the Fourth of July celebration. She and the committee had been working hard for months. I went to her kitchen and helped her bake five apple pies and five cherry pies as the big day drew nigh. She stayed up late making a huge German chocolate cake the night of July third. I sat at the table to keep her company long after Clay went to bed.

Clara bit her lip and stirred the chocolate. "Martha's on the program, you know."

I grated coconut. "Of course, I know. Your gang pasted handbills up all over town: HONORED GUEST: MARTHA MOODY, BELLE OF THE WEST."

"There's a reporter coming from the city. Martha's a big draw." Clara took the pan off the heat. "Will it upset you to see her?"

I shrugged. "If it does, I'll leave."

Mr. Henry, one of the other boarders, had requested that I accompany him to the barbecue and festivities. I told him I was not free to do so, but that I appreciated his courtesy. He bowed his shiny head and made no further inquiries.

The sun was bright the next day as I sat on a white blanket on the grass with Clay to watch the ceremonies. Clara was behind the bandshell, orchestrating the effects. There had been no parade this year, but we were to have speeches and a pageant and a presentation by Martha, then a barbecued chicken supper, with games. The chickens had been cooking slowly over fires all day, and the smell drifted across the park. People sat all around us in family groups. I saw Ruth at a distance, standing next to a small woman carrying a large basket. They were both surrounded by other brown-haired children, and Ruth was handing out peppermints to keep the kids from climbing their mother's skirts. I could see that one small girl was wearing the calico dress that Ruth had on when I first saw her running towards me across the back pasture. I waved, but she didn't see.

The Oddfellows Brass Band was tuning up, and I was surprised to see that John had taken his place in the front row with his horn. Clara had told me that John had stopped going to practices, preferring to wander about by himself playing his horn. He might have started rehearsing with them again when he had the place back. I didn't know. I hadn't spoken to John since I left the farm.

"Good crowd," said Clay, leaning back on his elbows. "I hope Clara doesn't bust a gut."

The band swung into Sousa, and the crowd cheered before they were through the first bar. The band was loud and stirring, and their instruments gathered the sun. A lady had put on her bonnet and blocked my view of John's face, but I imagined it intent, abandoned to pulling true notes out of himself to meld with those of his fellows, in a march that for the moment was the pleasure of the whole town. Clay was tapping one polished shoe, and everyone around me was smiling.

The band finished with sweeps and cymbals, then the Reverend came out to invoke God on the day. Most people bowed their heads or took sips of lemonade, but I looked straight at the dull man on the stage, and decided that I was seduced by the Bible, but not persuaded by God. I was ashamed of my own arrogance, but I had known ever since I first slept with Martha that I wasn't a Christian. Carry Nation had been right. I stopped listening, and looked at the tight weave of blue cotton over my own knees.

A bee landed near Clay's hand, and he brushed it away. Some children ran along the back of the crowd, throwing a potato from the barbecue coals and squealing. We all gave a little sigh as the Reverend said, "Amen."

The mayor said a few patriotic words. I thought about hearing the word Moody over and over and over. I was used to it: it was the name of my love, and it was where I was.

"Bit windy," said Clay. I knew he meant the mayor. The air was dry and still. The great bunches of ribbons tied to the bandstand by the committee women didn't stir. Not far from me, a little boy sat on an old blanket on top of an ice cream maker, while his father turned the crank.

The mayor moved the podium to one side when he was finished. A young man on the top of the bandshell dropped a green curtain. The band started to play.

Clay sat up and cracked his knuckles. "Here come the tableaux."

The young man hoisted the curtain, and everyone murmured. Martha was standing in the middle of the stage, striking an attitude with one hand behind her back and the other holding a large flag in the air. There was a sign on the stage in front of her that announced, "Liberty."

She was wearing a loose dress that flowed to her ankles with broad stripes of red and white and stripes of stars on blue.

She had a sash of the same material coming across one shoulder and tied at the opposite hip. Her hair was brushed up over her forehead and fell loose down her back like pure confusion. Pinned to her head at a jaunty angle was a top hat that was another flag. The brim was decorated with roses.

The band burst into "The Star-Spangled Banner" as she waved the flag over her head, then strode across the stage and stuck it in a stand. The crowd went wild, clapping and shouting and jumping to their feet. The band did the melody again, and the director turned to the people to lead them in song.

I put my head on my knees. Clay was standing. "By the dawn's early light." He looked down at me. "Aren't you feeling well?"

I kept my face to my skirt, and shook my head. Clay went on with the song. Martha was impressive in that costume, but I was sick with the feeling that I had been bought cheap. She could drape herself in flags and be Liberty. She could wash whiskey from my feet and be Mary anointing with sweet-smelling oils. She was a magnet for adulation. The feelings I had for her white, folding belly and her hands on my legs were jerked out of me like the frenzy of the crowd over red, white and blue.

I stretched out and put my face to the grass. The anthem ended. I looked up. Martha didn't smile or bow, but stood with her hand over her heart until the curtain went down.

I turned my head to tell Clay that I was just a little dizzy, and he sat down beside me and said, "Well, anything you need."

I propped my chin on my hands and stared at the rest of the pageant through the gaps between the bodies in front of me. Clara appeared as a dainty Betsy Ross, and Theda Wilks in a white wig got a hand as George Washington. I calmed as I watched them. I didn't lose any affection for Clara when I saw her showing her dimples in a rocking chair, stitching at a flag draped over her lap. Theda Wilks was twice as brazen as Martha in her satin knee pants and white stockings. But I still got a knot of fury when I thought of Martha marching across the stage in that get-up. It was like she was town property. What business did she have acting like that? She wasn't a young beauty: she was a fat storekeeper who dressed in black and showed her glamour only to me.

I sat up, churning and mourning and reasoning with myself while one student from each grade in Moody Grammar School did a recitation. The oldest was a pale girl in a pink bow who gave us "The Wreck of the Hesperus." Then the green curtain fell for the last time, and the mayor came out to announce that the dignitaries should come to the stage to honor Moody's founder and most famous daughter, Martha Moody.

The smoke from the barbecue thickened the air. I watched the Reverend and Martha's father climb the steps to the stage. Mr. Balm wore a white vest under his black coat, and his watch hung out of his pocket shimmering like the band's brass horns.

I had told Clara that I would leave if anything upset me, but I couldn't gather my feet under me, and there was no place for me to go. The thought of my room seemed repulsive, worse than seeing this out.

Martha entered last. She had taken off her patriotic costume and wore her black dress with the jet buttons down the front. She looked like a somber matron, except that she had on the satin bonnet that I had given her at the store one morning when I couldn't speak, long ago. I had meant her to run her hands over its soft surface and think of me. Now she had covered her red hair with it, and was standing before the crowd.

The mayor stood next to her to say that she needed no introduction, and that she would read a few lines of the famous stories that had brought such well-deserved attention to the town. He bowed himself back to his seat next to Martha's father, and they both crossed their legs and lit up cigars.

"Thank you." Martha held some pages in her hand, but she stood still and looked down at her feet for a few moments. The crowd gathered its attention around the bonnet's blank eye. I felt cold and hollow, like an empty pitcher in a springhouse.

Martha looked up, and began. "When Martha was a young woman, before she knew the extent of her powers, she wore trousers and swaggered on the dark, wooded lands of her father's estate. She carried her bow and arrow, but she was not a silent walker. She tromped and whistled at the birds to scare them. She scattered buckets of sunflower seed in winter in a clearing, so that when she burst into it, she would raise a crowd of wings."

I was shaking. I had never heard my writing aloud before. Martha was reading an unpublished story in a voice with ripples and currents. The crowd was silent, listening.

She went on. "Her father sometimes followed her with his soft, practiced step, standing back in the shadows to watch. He would time her progress with his gold watch, waiting for her to arrive at the river. He always gave up while she was still tromping through the woods, but he knew she went there, because he had looked out his window and seen the water change color. He had seen her footprints on the bank."

The mayor shifted, uncomfortable, but her father's expression didn't change. He kept his chin tilted into the air at an angle in a posture of proud attention, but I saw him move his hand to his vest and drop his gold watch into his pocket.

She spoke dreamily, as if telling a very old tale. "Martha's father was silent about what he wanted from her, but she was to marry wealth. That much was clear as consommé, and she had sucked it from her spoon since she was her mother's butterball. Her mother had been dead for many years."

Martha's voice fell into full quiet. No one else so much as coughed, but I stood up so I could see her clearly. Her face was shadowed by the bonnet, but her hands made small white movements in the afternoon air. I was mesmerized.

She read the rest of the story about a young woman whose father follows her into the woods, and a river that tries to help her by pouring water in her mouth. I saw her struggle in the waters. My anger dried. She gave me back my story with her own life moving in it. Watching her hands cup the meaning of the words, I felt seen and joined and understood.

On the dais, Martha's father gave a performance in coldness. He turned very white around the mouth, so that at a distance it looked like teeth were forming in his red cheeks, but he kept his head tilted as if rapt.

When she finished, Martha drew her hands down to her sides, subduing something. She took one step backwards, then lifted her shoulders and faced the crowd as if looking at them across the counter in her store.

Her father clapped strongly. I clapped, too, from where I stood near the back of the crowd. The people of Moody leaned on their hands, unsettled by hearing Martha describing herself in trousers and making strange revelations about social climbing and a father skulking in the bushes, so for a moment, it was just Martha's father and me applauding over their heads. But the mayor took it up quickly, and Clay stood up beside me, so the town rose to give an ovation.

Martha took off the bonnet and bowed. Her hair flashed, and the crowd warmed. They called her name. Mr. Balm stood beside her and hugged her shoulders. It struck me that he must have been the one who printed the placards and circulated Martha's picture, for as much as he hated the stories, he had slipped his pride into his pocket so he could share the acclaim.

Martha turned her shoulder against him and stepped free of his arm. She raised one hand for silence, and when it came, she said, "I'd like to introduce the author of these stories, Amanda Linger."

She pointed. Everyone stared. Clay took two steps away from me and sat down. I was trembling, but I waved at Martha and then to the crowd as they murmured and clapped.

Martha and the dignitaries left the stage. The mayor announced the crowning of the Butter Queen. Clay said, "Amanda, I had no idea."

I could see Clara, no longer Betsy Ross, making her way towards me through the crowd. Martha had walked to the edge of the park, and was speaking quietly with her father. He reached for her arm, but she held a distance he couldn't get across. Very young women in fancy dresses with bustles lined up on the stage.

I saw Clay's smile slough off in surprise as I turned and ran. Clara was waving her arm and calling my name. I bolted between the tables that the ladies were setting with platters of corn and potatoes, cold salads and rolls. I ran where the smoke was thickest, between the barbecue pits, where men were coughing with wet handkerchiefs over their mouths and turning the birds with long forks. I stopped next to three of them bending over one fire, and looked behind me. Clara was struggling to get between the tables and past the ladies with questions and compliments for her. Martha was coming, too. She had circled the crowd and was trying to find me in the smoke.

My heart was pounding. I knew I couldn't keep running long. I made a move towards Martha, but then I saw that she had pursuers of her own. A mob of children caught up with her, waving *True Western Tales*. Ruth was with them, swinging her little sister off the ground by one hand.

I took off down Main Street as fast as I could. My holiday slippers were flapping, so I kicked them off and ran in my stockings. I passed the church and the station and Moody's Store. I could hear the feet behind me. My bonnet fell and I left it on the ground. I crossed the edge of town, and turned towards the stream.

I was flying, truly frightened, although I couldn't say what of. The footsteps were loud and close behind me. There were many of them, shaking the grasses with their pounding. Then the first one came alongside me, a boy in his Sunday suit who gave me a grin. His legs were pumping, and his long bangs flew back across his eyes. He passed me and kept running to the line of cottonwoods that marked the water.

They were all around me—girls in stiff dresses, girls in light dresses, boys in dungarees and knickers and caps. They were sprinting for the water as if we had decided to play this game instead of the egg toss and the three-legged race.

My breath clattered against the bones of my chest, but I kept running as fast as I could. The children passed me easily as wind bent the grasses. I didn't mind them, but I heard heavier footsteps behind me.

Ruth caught me. She had let go of her sister. "Hey, Mrs. Linger!" she shouted, and kept going.

The sight of Ruth's clean running stride cut through me, and suddenly I wasn't afraid. I saw the hill behind Clara's place in the distance, and let out a howl. Birds were scaring up out of the grass in front of me, ahead of the children. The trees were dancing closer and closer. The kids were climbing trees and throwing rocks into the water. I passed between two cottonwoods and put my palms flat on their bark to steady myself, then I stepped off the bank into the stream.

It was cold and shallow. The rocks were sharp, but then I found a muddy place to stand. The water splashed up around me. Ruth was in the water. She kicked a wave at me, laughing, then all of the children piled in from the bank. The boy in his Sunday suit took his clothes off, and hung them in a tree, so he was soaked in his drawers. We kicked that water into foam, and it skimmed cold up our legs. I bent over and ducked my hair in the water, then shook it in the air. I was screeching, but the children were as loud.

I saw Martha reach the bank. She looked down at us a moment, then sat down on the edge, and slid through the mud into the water. The back of her skirt was smeared with brown. "You've got mud on your skirt!" I shouted, and she sat down in the water.

Martha bellowed with cold and kicked her feet. I waded through children splashing like fountains, and helped her to unlace her boots.

"Can't I keep my dignity?" asked Martha from the water.

When I bent to hand her boot back to her, she emptied it over my head.

"Baptism!" hollered Clara, as dry and pink as ever. She was leaning against a willow, holding Ruth's little sister by the hand.

"Ma will be mad!" yelled the girl to everyone. We all slapped water in that direction, and drenched her and Clara both.

Martha tossed her boots onto the bank. "Might as well come on in, Mrs. Spencer. You're wet enough as it is."

Clara smiled and shook her head. "Someone has to keep an eye on the children." She sat on the bank, took off her shoes and stockings, and dangled her feet into the water. The little girl waded in, but she kept hold of Clara's hand.

Martha made great circular splashes with her free arm, drenching the children and the trees. I spun around with her, slipping and laughing and holding on tight.

The children started diving for the brightest stones. Martha and I walked upstream. Our feet were numb. The water ran between us. Our dresses clung to the stays of Martha's corset and the folds of my belly falling loose. The children were shouting, but I could hear the wind rustling every leaf and the talk of the stream as it passed deeper and deeper between the banks.

We stopped walking when we reached a patch of mud. Martha let go of my hand and stepped away from me. She tilted her head as if she were about to speak, then raised water cupped in both hands and splashed it in her own face.

"I've missed you," she said, streaming.

I felt breathless, and almost absent. I wished this were a story so my chest would open like a flower, and I would toss her petals from my heart. Instead I wiped my face on my dripping sleeve, and said, "Then why didn't you come?"

Martha shook her head so fiercely that her hair fell from its pins. Spray enclosed her in a quick sphere of light. She said, "I thought you understood."

She stood there with her legs planted and her skirt moving in the water, looking as full of power as John the Baptist ready to dunk Jesus in the river Jordan. I gazed at her, and I didn't understand.

"Why couldn't you? What stopped you?" The water was lapping at my calves.

Martha's face drooped and strained. She turned away from me and took a few thrashing steps upstream. She was kicking the water, and there was no joy in it. I dug my feet deeper into the mud.

She put her hand on the bank and turned to me. "I lost everything twice. When I left the city with my husband. When I stopped here, and let Wilbur go on." She met my eyes. "I'm so scared to risk all that again."

Her voice was blunt. I looked at her rising up out of the water, and she throbbed in the air with a beat like a bird leaving a tree. I wanted to wash her out of my life. I wanted to lie on the bank with her and press my voice into her mouth. I thought of everything I had lost since I had brought her that one bottle of stolen wine, and I dropped to my knees in the water. I thought to tear at my clothes and eat mud, but just knelt.

Martha kept talking. She said again that she was afraid, and she said that she was lost. She said her father's name, Mr. Balm. She talked about missing me every night in her bed over the store, and the moments in the day when she poured beans into the barrel or passed the butter case, and how she watched what Ruth bought every week. She never spoke to the girl.

Martha said that when she heard Miss Alice had died, she had walked out to my house carrying my dusty bottle of wine in a burlap sack, as a gift. She had come to my door, knocked, walked in, and found no one at home. She had sat at my kitchen table, eaten a cold piece of corn bread, wiped up the crumbs and left. She had wanted to leave a note, but didn't have a pen. She kept the wine because she didn't want to give me the shock of finding it without knowing what it meant: that it was an offering, not a casting off.

I watched her mouth. Martha said she had studied the stories. She didn't like all of them, but she loved some. She said she had chosen the one she read at the pageant today because it was true.

She came back towards me, walking more softly in the water. I stood up. She was quiet for a moment, then said, "I'm sorry, Amanda."

I put my hand on her dripping waist, shaking with things to tell her and ask her and shout at her about. How could she leave me alone for so long? How could she let her father stand at the counter of her store? Why had she named me to the crowd without a single word of preparation or permission between us? What would she have been risking to gather her skirts in her fist and cross the road to see me at the boarding house?

There was more, but I didn't speak. Martha was looking at me with eyes as sharp and stunning as they had been the first time I had spotted her in the creek. Downstream, I could see Clara helping Ruth's little sister out of the water and drying the girl's small feet on her apron.

I followed Martha's eyebeams back to her face, and felt led out of the wilderness. Martha was in the stream with me. She was sorry. We had the possibility of grace between us.

I said, "I'm so thirsty."

She plunged both hands into the water, then held them out to me. I bent to her palms, and drank like a cow at the trough.

Fourteen

That evening I climbed out onto the boarding house roof to watch the fireworks. Martha, the honored guest, had to light the first fuses, but she would come to my room through the unlocked kitchen door after the show was over.

As I settled myself on the shingles, holding my skirt at the knees, I could see "STAPLES AND FANCY GROCERIES" painted bold so that it stood out on the side of her store in the fading light. I could see the railroad station and the staked-off field where the people of Moody were sitting on the ground, looking up. They made a beautiful pattern with their blankets and quick darting children, but I had no desire to be among them. Their voices closed into one sound that was almost a hush, but if I went down there, they would speak around me in the old harsh-edged whispers.

I had left Clara and Martha in the center of town with the straggling group of children returning from the creek. Women in groups and pairs were coming away from the fires to meet the children. Clara squeezed my hand and waded in. "Oh, hello, Dora, got all that potato salad ready? Yes, I've been watching them. Here's Seth, all in one piece. Wet, I know, but it's such a hot day. Need help cutting up chicken, Opal? Let me have a word with Clay, and I'll be right there."

The women surrounded her, waving fans and meat tongs, drawing her towards the smoking pits. I saw Ruth scanning the crowd. When she spotted her mother, she ran to hug her with a wet, smacking sound, tugging her little sister by the hand as if she had never let go.

Martha whispered, "Tonight," in my ear, then skirted the crowd of women, her wet dress leaving a swatch of bent grass as she hurried past the picnic grounds towards the bandshell.

I had gone up to my room, put on dry clothes, and sat down with my notebook, but I couldn't write. I was restless. I dusted the bureau and changed my sheets. There was no one else in the boarding house. When I opened the window and sat down on the sill to comb out my hair, I could smell the smoke drifting from the barbecue pits.

Martha had left me alone because she had been afraid of what she was risking by wanting me. She had been a walking psalm to me, my body of courage, but she couldn't be all that to herself. She had inspired me, so that I could go to town without my corset and sell butter and leave John. I wondered how she saw me. I had built a vision of Martha in her absence, and I knew that it was part remembered sex and part dream and part real. The real part was becoming insistent. I thought of how scared Martha must have been to say my name in front of the whole gathered town, and how clear her voice had been as she had called it out. I heard it again, and I shook with drastic love.

I stood up and began to circle the room. I wanted to see her, right then. I knew she was being celebrated and attended to by her father and Theda Wilks and all of the dignitaries of the town, but I wondered if she had changed from her wet clothes. There would be no question of surrendered dignity if she had not, but when the day finally gave way to evening, she might get cold.

I opened the bureau and took out my wool shawl. I would find her in a quiet moment, give her the shawl, and slip away. She could wear it to be warm beneath the fireworks, and pull it around her later as she made her way to me.

The afternoon was lingering as I approached the back of the bandshell through the makeshift lot where country people in for the day had left their wagons and carriages. I thought I could stand behind the green curtain and peer at the field covered with families eating chicken and sweet corn. Martha was usually easy to spot.

I saw her father while I was still among the wagons, so I crouched down next to a wheel. He was sitting on a stump with his head in his hands. Martha stood in front of him, still as a pillar of salt. She was not nodding or touching his shoulder, but she seemed to be listening. I couldn't hear their words. The late afternoon light slanted and broke over the tight roll of her hair. She had changed her dress.

Martha had no need for the dry shawl folded over my arm, but I did not retreat. It looked to be a delicate moment. I watched.

He stood up abruptly, taller than her, though not by much. I marked the distance between his high belly under its vest and her urgent figure pushing against laces and whale bone as she faced him. His head jerked as he spoke, and his finger jabbed the air.

She grabbed his watch chain. I saw it gleaming in her fingers, and his sudden fists. I rose from behind the wagon wheel, but there was no other motion. She stood with the watch and chain pooled in her hands. He waited with his own hands in knots, not moving. I reached into the bed of the wagon and took hold of a shovel.

Martha took a step back from him and tossed the watch in the air. She caught it on her fingers, then twirled it. He spoke to her again, his eyes on her face. I thought she was going to throw the watch into the grasses and dust, but she opened her palm and stopped it neatly in mid-swing. He pretended to clap, but she grabbed his wrist with her empty hand. His face was blood-red, and I moved closer.

Martha stood back from her father and pressed the watch to his heart. She ground it against him with the heel of her hand then let it drop. He caught it above his knees.

He shook it at her, furious. She showed him her empty hands and lifted her chin. The chain cut the air in front of her.

She said, "Stop." I saw her mouth move.

He stopped, then put the watch in his pants pocket. They stood looking at each other, just as before, except that Mr. Balm's shoulders were shaking. He sat back down on the stump. I rested the shovel on the ground. Martha wiped her face with the back of her hand, then wiped her hands on her skirt.

Theda Wilks came striding past the bandshell wearing green silk and a big hat. She walked right up to Martha, laughing and waving a small piece of white rope. Martha looked at Theda, then looked at her father. She rocked on her hips, and motion rippled over her. She offered her father her hand. He took it, and got up off the stump, but I could see something had shifted.

Martha turned and swept back towards the crowd with her pride loose in her walk. Theda hurried after her, and her father followed more slowly.

I put the shovel back in the wagon, and returned to my room to wait.

Soon after I got there and sat down on the bed, there was a knock at my door. Clara had sent a little boy over with a plate of chicken, bean salad and a big slice of her German chocolate cake, along with a note telling me that Martha and Theda Wilks had won the three-legged race, and were now picnicking with her father at the mayor's table. Clara thought the whole party seemed to be in good spirits.

I gave the boy a penny and shut the door. I had been born with patience and a steady stomach, so I ate the food and carried the plate down to the kitchen to rinse it. I unlocked the kitchen door so Martha could get in when she was ready, then climbed the stairs to the top floor and took the ladder that led to the roof. I wanted to see the fireworks.

I had a long wait in the dusk. The sky turned deep blue, then paled again before it shifted into dark. The town was quiet. The first burst came a long time before any of the others. One white line shot up from the horizon, then opened into a ball that spilled out with quick lavender spokes running from the center.

I gasped. It was so large and bright. While it still lit the sky, I saw a small figure coming down the street, waving a sparkler. I squinted my eyes until I could see her skinny legs and wild hair. It was Ruth.

She sat down on the porch steps of the store, humming to herself and looking up. The whole sky was reflected in the plate glass window, with the painted letters, MOODY'S, outlined under the splashes of light. The fireworks were coming steadily: blue, green, then the loud bang. Orange uncurled into fingers that became crackling points of light. Firewheels faded into bright red balls. A fountain spouted colors from the ground.

Ruth's sparkler went out. She struck a match, lit a firecracker, and tossed it into the air. It exploded with a barking pop. High above her, something gold took shape in the air, swelled like a breast or a fruit rounding out. It was huge. Far beneath it, Ruth lit a new sparkler with a tiny flame.

She stood and danced on the porch, waving the sparkler in loops and circles. The light doubled in the reflection from the storefront window. I clapped and called the name of Salome, a dancer in the Bible. Ruth was just a skinny little girl playing with paths of light. She had already slipped three matches and a burned-out sparkler between the porch slats. When I yelled from the roof, she dropped the lit one, and something dry caught.

Ruth jumped off the porch and stood in the middle of Main Street. "Who's that?" she called, half crouched and ready to run.

I waved my arm, not sure if she could see me. "It's me. Amanda Linger. On the roof."

She squinted at me, and I saw relief in the way she let her shoulders drop before I saw the smoke pouring out from under the porch behind her. Before I could understand what was happening, flames were licking between the slats.

"Oh. Mrs. Linger. Hi." Ruth was twisting her fingers in her hair, embarrassed.

The fire behind her covered the steps. I found myself shouting. "The porch is on fire! Get folks to come. Now!"

Ruth swung to look behind her and yelled, "Sweet Jesus!" She took off towards the picnic grounds in a flat-out run.

I waited a moment longer, staring at the fireworks as if I thought that Martha would come from the sky riding Miss Alice to save her worldly goods. Then I felt the urgency of reality, and flew down the ladder and the stairs. I filled buckets in the kitchen and ran out the door.

It had been a dry summer, and the porch was burning in a high, steady flame. I threw one bucket of water on the fire, and there was a hiss, but I saw that I was already too late. I ran around the back of the building, through the garden, and tried the back door. It was locked. I threw a rock through the kitchen window, wild with the idea that there was something inside I had to save, but the broken pane was small and jagged with glass. A blast sent me backing across the garden. A keg of kerosene had gone up.

When I circled to the front of the store, people were running from the picnic grounds—families who had been on the far edge of the crowd, men sweating in their holiday clothes, Theda Wilks on her white horse. When they reached the store, they stopped and threw their heads back to find the top of the flames. People touched each other's shoulders, then turned home for buckets and shovels. Martha's near neighbors ran to their wells and started to pump.

Martha arrived running slow-footed through the crowd. Before she was within breathing distance of the heat, she was gathering people into lines from pumps to the store. She raised her arm, drew a column in the air, and people filled it in with their full buckets and their bent backs.

Theda tied her horse to the post in front of the bank, then ran over to shovel dirt on the smoldering boards of the porch. I saw John standing in mud past his ankles, pumping water. The sheriff conferred with Martha, then took a group of men to wet down the buildings on either side of the store.

Her father wrapped his arms around her and tried to pat her head. "My poor child. All we had, lost." Martha suffered him for a moment, then put him to work.

I passed buckets until my hands blistered, then bled, and Moody's store was collapsed into hot ash on the ground. None of the other buildings burned, but nothing of Moody's was saved. Even Martha's garden had been tromped on, and its beautiful rows of red cabbages were broken.

Martha stood in front of what was left of the porch, with its crumbled steps and the gray-hot hoops of the cracker barrels heaped at her feet. The women of the town looked up, dropped their buckets and pressed in on all sides of her, me along with the others, as she swayed there, her air of command draining from her like water from a sink. Her father watched, fingering the fabric of his coat, as Martha bit her lip and trembled. We led her away.

Martha disappeared into Theda Wilks's large house. I woke up late in the morning after the fire to whispering in the boarding house hall.

"The sheriff says fireworks, but I think Mrs. Linger set it. She was already there when we came running, with an evil smile on her face, and you heard that Carry Nation called her a heathen."

"Land no, I hadn't heard that. But she's always been unfriendly, and of peculiar appearance."

"She only recently started washing."

"No."

"Yes. And Martha Moody had unmasked her that very day."

"You mean about the stories."

"Quite sensational, most of them. No wonder she didn't give her name."

I threw my pillow at the door as hard as I could, and heard them gasp at the thump, and scurry away.

I lay there flat on the mattress for a moment, rubbing my thumb across the blisters on my palm. I felt like crying, but I was too tired to get up any tears. That silly scrap of gossip gnawed at me. I felt grief for Martha, and also shifty and ashamed.

I dressed and went out to circle the ruins of the store, hoping to see Martha or Ruth. The sheriff had posted a deputy to keep folks from taking anything they might find, but he didn't stop Martha's father from poking through the ashes. When Mr. Balm saw me, he narrowed his eyes. I turned and left him to his scavenging.

I walked out to a small, gray farmhouse with the yard full of dogs and children, still looking for Ruth. I found her mother in the kitchen, dusting great balls of dough with flour. She wiped her hands on her apron and told me that Ruth had left the house before dawn that morning. "She brought the children home while I was helping put out the fire, and she was sitting on the edge of her bed when I finally got in. She was watching the kids and worrying, I expect. I had her lie down and pulled the covers up over her, but when I got up this morning, she was gone." She had rolled the dough flat, and was cutting out biscuits with a jelly jar. "If I didn't know better, I'd have thought she was at your old place playing with that cow of yours that died."

I thanked her and stuck my lips sideways and crossed my eyes for the children, then walked up the lane. Ruth could be sitting in the hayloft of John's barn, or next to Miss Alice's grave, or a hundred other places that a girl from a crowded house with a feeling for privacy would know, but I took the path to the creek.

I waded the water with a sharp eye to the bank until I spotted the split roots of the big willow that framed her hiding hole. From a short distance I could see the tight curve of her back, covered with blue calico. She looked a little like an animal new to the world, and a lot like a miserable girl.

"Ruth," I said, "come out. It's me, Amanda."

Her back kept its blue-flowered curve, and I was frightened by how still she was. I put a hand on each root and leaned into the hole. "Ruth, can you hear me? Are you okay?"

She turned onto her belly and crawled farther back into the hole, so I lost sight of her back and found her shadowed face. "I'm sorry," she whispered. "I didn't mean for anything to burn."

"Oh, Ruth." I leaned down to her and she grabbed my arms at the elbows as I lifted her from the hole.

She was smeared with dirt and crying. The shame on her face was so much harder for me to look at than the grief we had felt together when Miss Alice died, that I stuck my head in the hole, and said, "Now I want to crawl in."

Ruth rinsed her hands and legs in the water. "You'll never fit."

I turned and looked at her, dirt crumbling into my hair. "It wasn't your fault, Ruth. It was an accident. I saw it all."

She rubbed the back of one hand on her leg and let out a lungful of old air. "What should I do?"

I shrugged my shoulders, which brought a shower of dirt into my face. I offered her the rock of fantasy. "What would Queen Jezebel do?"

Theda herself answered the door. She took hold of my arm and pulled me inside. Ruth followed with her eyes on the rose carpet. She had on a clean dress with her hair tightly braided, but she stuck her hands in her pockets and bunched her dress together in the front.

Theda let go of me in the hall, and hooked her thumbs in her black sash. She looked as uncomfortable as Ruth. They didn't seem to see each other, but Ruth edged closer to me as Theda leaned on the door.

"We want to see Martha," I said.

Theda sighed and reknotted the sash. "Maybe you can help."

She led us upstairs to a dark bedroom, where Martha curled up under the covers like Ruth in her hole. She looked at us without interest. I stared at her for a moment as I had stared at the sky when her store caught fire, then I crossed the room and reached under the quilt for her hand.

She didn't move away. Her fingers gripped mine, but it seemed involuntary, like a pea vine curling around a piece of chicken wire. I dug my other hand into her hair as if I could comb through her listlessness with my bare fingers. Theda brought me a brush without being asked, and she and Ruth watched while I brushed Martha's matted hair.

Martha didn't flinch. She didn't turn, and she didn't talk. After her glance as we walked in the door, she looked past us toward the bureau. I could see her eyes moving, as if she were tracing the lines of the drawer handles.

"Martha," I said softly, "Martha, you must be so sad." I pulled the brush through her hair as gently as I knew how. Martha either didn't hear me, or didn't care enough to let me know she had, and her fingers were falling like stones from my other hand.

I heard a stifled noise. It was Theda crying. Tears were dripping off the end of her nose, and she had taken her sash off and wrapped it around her fists. Martha turned her face to the pillow. Ruth was standing stiffly next to the bureau, her hands clasped in front of her as if someone had told her to take them out of her pockets.

"Ruth," I said. She offered me her young, determined face. "Go down to the store and see if Martha's father is there. If he is, try to get him away. Tell him the banker sent you to find him. Tell him anything."

Theda wiped her nose on her sleeve. "I'll go. He'll listen to me."

I worked a snarl with the brush, trying not to tug at the roots. Martha didn't blink. "Good. Get rid of the deputy, too."

Theda nodded and walked to the door. She stopped, turned to me, and said, "What will you be doing?" in a thick, uncertain voice. I took another stroke. "Martha and I will meet you at the store."

———

Ruth waited downstairs while I got Martha into her clothes. It was easier than I had expected. Martha stayed sitting up when I pushed at her shoulders, and was silently cooperative as I helped her dress. If she hadn't been willing to stand, Ruth and I never could have moved her. Martha was a woman of substance, even with her glance reduced to smoke.

As we walked to the store with Martha's arm around my shoulder and Ruth's arm around her waist, I felt as if Main Street were burning under my feet. I wanted to take Martha alone with me down to the water, and try to cool her grief and her skin. I wanted to tongue her dry, as if that could be her saving grace, but Martha wasn't with me in that way. I couldn't do her an evil by trying to join our bodies when her face was so helpless and her walk so slack.

"What are we going to do?" Ruth asked from under Martha's other arm.

"I don't know," I said. Martha gave a soft, harsh sigh, but I wasn't sure if she was listening. My only idea was to look through the ashes with Martha and try to see what could be saved.

When we got to the ruin, we didn't see Martha's father or the deputy, but the store cat Bathsheba was curled up on a loose heap. I recognized it by pieces of charred walnut as Martha's bed.

The cat got up and strutted over to us, purring. Martha sat down in the ashes, and Bathsheba climbed into her lap. I watched Martha stroke the cat, and remembered the pane I had broken out of the kitchen window. That might have been how Bathsheba got out. I stood with my hand on Martha's head, and Ruth squatted down a little distance away, her eyes to the ground.

Theda approached with the church ladies' committee. Clara told me later that they had been having an emergency meeting when they saw Theda running towards the burned store. They came up very quietly for women whose lifeblood was talk. When I thought about it, I realized that the group might have included whoever had been gossiping outside my door, but it didn't matter. Clara had given Theda her shawl. She nodded to me, and I felt a jolt of love. They stood around me and Martha, ready to witness and to help.

I looked at Theda, and she said, "They're at the bank, talking about capital loans."

I nodded, then knelt down next to Martha, and said, "I'm going to start digging, and I'm not going to stop until I find something you still want."

She kept stroking the cat, her face towards her lap. I picked up a slender piece of burnt wood. I looked at it a while before I knew what it was. I nodded when I got it, and dug around for the blade.

"What is it?" Martha asked me.

"Axe handle," I told her, and set it aside.

We did this for a long time. The other women helped, finding spoons and pliers. They brought everything to me, and then Martha asked what it was. I told her all we found.

When Ruth dug up an unbroken glass jar full of peppermints, she brought them to us with her lip gnawed under her teeth. She sat with the jar next to Martha, then started crying.

"I'm sorry," she said, "I'm so sorry. It was an accident. A sparkler. I'm sorry." The women stopped working to listen.

Martha looked up, unsmiling. Ruth's lip was bleeding. Martha took the lid off the jar and offered her a peppermint.

"Here," she said. "No charge."

Ruth stopped sobbing and took the candy. She looked at it seriously, then placed it in her mouth. She didn't say thank you.

Martha nodded once. "Pass the candy around." Then she looked at me. "Tell me what burned."

So the women sucked hard candy and kept digging while I told Martha what she had lost. She knew, but I named things: the licorice, the salt pork, the pepper, the yard goods, the butter case, the magazines, and the office door, although we found the yellow glass with "OFFICE" written in gilt. The counter was gone. Her Shakespeare upstairs and her bed were burnt. All the barrels were lost to the fire: potatoes, grains, onions, molasses, kerosene. Brooms, matches, lanterns, fly paper, cinnamon and mustard were lost. The cash register could be recognized, and might be cleaned to work. The painted basin where she had washed my feet was cracked into shards too small to piece back.

The women listened and made nodding sounds as they reached under half-burnt beams. Martha cried with her head in my lap. It was as if we were casting a spell on her despair, turning it into something made of food, wood, metal and feathers; something we could clean.

When Martha started screaming, the sound washed over me like splashes of water or washes of fire. The cat left her, suddenly wild. Martha got to her feet. She started throwing and scattering the things we had salvaged. She pounded the yellow glass with a hunk of metal. She smashed the peppermint jar.

The women stepped back into a loose circle. Martha kicked into the rubble and raised a cloud of ash. She lifted the cash register over her head and heaved it into what was left of a wall. She was wailing and grunting, and I could see half-circles of sweat darkening her dress.

Men came running from all directions, drawn, as always, by noise and dust, but the women held them back. Clara seized Mr. Balm by his coattails, and even he did not advance. She told me later that the men said Martha and I were staggering drunk. They said we held lit matches to hundred-dollar bills and poured bottles of whiskey over each other's heads.

I didn't notice that the town was gathering and murmuring under floating bits of ash. I had my whole mind on Martha as she stomped on a wrecked barrel. I did see Dora Hassett out of the corner of my eye as she slipped a handful of blackened thimbles into her pocket, but I paid her no mind, because Martha suddenly stopped screeching and charged one end of the circle of people, as if she wanted to bolt and run.

Both Clara and the sheriff stepped back, so Martha had openings, but she veered away and ran back to the middle of the ruin. She stood there, panting.

I walked slowly towards her. Her face was red and swollen, her hands were filthy. I wasn't calm or clean, either, but she fastened her eyes on me. "Amanda," she said, "I'm lost."

She sat down in the mess, and I sat down with her. She trembled and held me, and the people moved farther away from her grief. I think they started to leave then. I think Clara urged them along, but I put my face in Martha's hair and shook with her, so I didn't see.

After a long while, she started whispering to me. She said things were awful, awful, then she told me that when she was a girl, when she had been worn out from archery and swimming and still had an empty afternoon, she used to sit on the lawn and say verses from Shakespeare over and over. She said it wasn't from love of language, but because her father had told her that this was the greatest writer that ever lived, and she thought she better know what he said, in case her father's house and the servants were ever lost. She said she had known how close she was to having nothing on those afternoons, and she had been trying to find things she could keep.

I kept my arms around her and my head down close to hear, but I had to turn away to cough from the ash.

Martha said, "I used my store of verses in the dry days walking across the plains with Wilbur. I played long passages over and over in my mind. I used it the first winter in the sodhouse. Sometimes I would laugh from the clash between where I was and what was humming in my head. I went back to the book to find more." She smoothed a small burnt mound with her toe. "I can't remember any of it now."

Martha sat up and turned her face to me. I felt as if her eyes were drawing words out of me. She wanted them and was looking for them and I had some inside me. I didn't have any Shakespeare, but I put my hand on her cheek, and said, "And suddenly there came a sound from heaven as of a rushing mighty wind, and it filled all the house where they were sitting. And there appeared unto them cloven tongues like as of fire, as it sat upon each of them. And they were all filled with the Holy Ghost, and began to speak with other tongues, as the Spirit gave them utterance."

Martha sat very still and listened. She watched my mouth for a moment after I stopped, then she hugged me with an intensity that made me feel I wrote the Bible.

"It's Acts," I told her, coughing again. "The Pentecost."

Martha felt in her pockets, then got to her feet. "I don't have a handkerchief," she said. She took my hands and helped me up.

I looked around, a little dazed, and saw a small group clumped at the edge of the road, looking at us. Clara was there, and Ruth and Theda, Martha's father, and some others. Martha saw them too, and sighed, then wiped her hands on her skirt and said, "I better go show them I've got my sense."

She touched my arm and started towards them, then stopped and turned back to me. "Those are pearls that were her eyes."

Her voice was soft, but it surged.

Fifteen

We formed a travelling snake-oil show. Martha sold pork 'n' beans and elixirs from the side of the wagon during the day, and performed tales from her storied past from the back at night. I packed and cooked and wrote by the campfire. At first I felt confined sleeping in the wagon with Martha snoring beside me, but I learned to take my blanket out under the stars when I needed room. She didn't like to wake up by herself without knowing that I was gone, so I tucked the quilt around her shoulders and told her I was leaving before I climbed out the back. She would raise herself sleepily up on one elbow and kiss me goodnight. We made bad mistakes before we learned our habits of tenderness.

Sometimes, as I lay on my back tracing the slow spin of the constellations, I remembered slipping away nights from the bed I had shared with John. Then I had felt hunched and furtive. Now I was open to the whole sky. My eyes could leap the dark from Cassiopeia to the North Star to the pointer in the handle of the Big Dipper, and on to Boötes and Virgo and all of the Greek stories that hovered in their light.

People bought our wares. They had heard of Martha and favored her over local stores, especially for volatile things such as herbs and kerosene. She carried her clippings and stacks of back issues of *True Western Tales,* which sold well to the children, who still asked her to sign the garish covers. Martha stood beneath the pans hanging from the roof of the wagon, looking businesslike, but when she played herself from the gate that unlatched into a small wooden stage, she was so luminous that anyone could see straight through her black dress to the dark wagon and the night sky behind her.

I loved to watch her shine. I sat behind a collapsible table at the back of the crowd, selling fruit and magazines, as Martha floated my stories out over the edge of the kerosene stagelights to the people who had come to listen. She offered them stories with small, agile enhancements from her hips and her hands. Young girls became voracious for apples while Martha performed. They bought them for each other, eating slowly, but to the core.

Buck and Bob pulled the wagon. They were both strong horses, middling young, red and husky with dark manes that Martha kept cropped. Martha loved the horses, and I considered them friends, but if I spoke to them, it was only about distance and grasses and water and oats. If I had a yen for cooking in a real kitchen or a dream about my dead, I told Martha. She listened with a calm that reminded me strangely of Miss Alice, but she had strictly human ways of remembering other dreams I had forgotten, finding wild onions for the pan-fried potatoes, and saying my name.

We rode long miles together, silent and talking. On empty stretches, when Buck and Bob knew she couldn't mean them to turn, Martha would touch my cheek with the edge of the reins, and I would turn my head and open my mouth to taste her fingers and the leather. Or I rubbed her shoulders as she drove.

She had built special drawers into the wagon to hold my papers and my sewing and my pens. I had told her every memory I had of my mother, and she had told me amazing events that had occurred in each year of her life.

Her presence echoed in everything I wrote, but I never caught her in all her complexity. I made up stories about children I saw in the towns and the conversations I had with their mothers regarding changes in the weather and the best spice for rabbit stew. I wrote in every language the land spoke to me, which was mostly motion, smells, and lines of light.

All of this went into the stories about the other, mythic Martha that I wrote for our steady money. Frank Sibsen sent the checks in care of Clara at her farm. Over the years we settled into a circuit of towns, although sometimes we reversed ourselves, or took a figure-eight path of travel instead of a loop. We never went too far east. Clara sent the checks to us general delivery in towns on our path, with recipes for dried meat and sage poultices in her tight, looping hand.

It was a good life, and we formed friendships in the towns we passed through. One woman in Arthur always asked us to sleep for a week in her spare room because she wanted us to remember what it was like to live indoors. Her bed was too soft, but she played the fiddle in the parlor, and let me make a mess in her big kitchen, then clean the dishes in water from the garden pump.

Once a year we went back and camped at the foot of Clara's hill. Clara came running out of her kitchen door, waving wildly as we followed Buck and Bob up the path to the house. She threw her arms around me and hugged me tight, small woman that she was. I loved the smells of vanilla and woodsmoke in her hair.

One year, Martha hung back, unhitching the horses, but Clara took a bridle so she could squeeze Martha's hand. "Do you want the spare room? There's cold meat and pie, but if I had known you were coming, I would have baked a cake."

Martha and I welcomed the chance to sit down at Clara's table, but we didn't take her offer of a room. In Moody, we both preferred the wagon to a house.

Clay welcomed us warmly, as always, and gave the horses clean stalls in the barn with his mules. Ruth burst into the kitchen and hugged me before she sat down to the meal. Clay had hired her to help him work the farm instead of his usual boy. She wore her hair in a bun, but she still got excited over the odd stones I gathered for her along the road.

After we ate and gossiped, Martha borrowed the desk in the study to add checks from Frank Sibsen and go over our accounts from the past year. Ruth took my arm and led me to the pasture past Clay's barn. She rattled the gate, and a black-and-white cow hustled up to the fence.

Ruth reached into a pocket of her work jacket and offered a handful of oats. She looked at me as the cow ate from her hand. "This is Jezebel. Do you like her?"

I felt an ache sharper than the one I got every year when Clara and I walked the back path between her land and my old place, holding hands. I never went to the house or visited John, but I would stand with Clara at the edge of the pasture and look at the barn and past it to the line of trees that marked the creek. Now I reached out and patted this cow's warm neck. "She sure is pretty, Ruth. Is she yours?"

Ruth scratched under Jezebel's chin. "I bought her with savings from my wages. She's a good milker."

I looked full at Ruth, with her long legs and her new woman's hips, and asked, "Do you ever ride her?"

Ruth tossed another shower of oats over the fence. "In my dreams."

We didn't say the name of Miss Alice. We leaned towards each other, and laughed.

Martha and I went into town that afternoon. She walked up Main Street with a large stride, as if she had never left. I hurried beside her, wrapped in my best shawl.

The new store was brick, but it stood on the same lot, and said "MOODY'S" over the door. Mr. Balm had rebuilt. It smelled very much like the inside of our wagon when we walked in the door.

Martha nodded at the thick-necked boy behind the counter, then started wandering the aisles. The clerk blinked and called, "Mr. Balm! Mr. Balm?"

Martha's father came from the back office with the solid wood door, and rubbed the tops of Martha's arms with both hands, in way of welcome. He bowed cordially to me. His gold watch gleamed on his chest as brightly as ever, although Clara said it had disappeared when Mr. Balm was borrowing money to rebuild the store.

He took us out to lunch at the new restaurant, and ordered chicken with all the fixings. We talked trade and inventory, and he let us know that he was doing mighty well. Then he said, "I've been having troubling dreams." He picked up his fork. "Daughter, stay home with me."

I ate tapioca pudding while Martha shook her head.

———

That evening evening Ruth stopped Martha and me as we walked towards our camp. She offered us a small bowl.

"Try this on your biscuits in the morning," she said. "It's from Jezebel."

Martha raised the lantern, so we could see what Ruth held out. The smooth mound of butter shone under the flickering light.

Martha took the bowl. "Thank you."

Ruth turned and ran back towards the lit barn, calling goodnight. She still had a beautiful run.

Martha and I talked a little as we walked down the hill, of how tall and serious Ruth had gotten, of how good it had been to see Clara in the yard as we came up, tiny bows fluttering all over her bodice and sleeves as she waved. We didn't speak of the first butter I had brought to Martha, hidden under my shawl. We were careful, when we were in Moody, not to tell each other too many stories.

It was a cool night, but we were camped in the shelter of the hill. Martha had lit a fire in the wood stove before it had gotten dark, so the wagon was warm. I set the bowl of butter on the roof of the wagon, where it would be safe from prowling animals, and climbed in. I changed out of my travelling dress into my loose nightgown, and got under the covers.

When Martha stepped up over the back gate, she brought some kindling for the fire, and the butter. She stacked the wood by the stove in the corner, then sat down on the covers beside me, rolling the butter over and over in her hands, until her palms slipped and shone. I sat up and pulled the nightgown off over my head. The metal of the stove was glowing red. I held out my hand for the butter.

Martha gave it to me, then pulled her hands down the soft slopes of my back. "Amanda," she said, "we lost so much."

I started to answer, but she put her hand to my mouth. I tasted it, then started crying, but the feeling was nothing I would call pain. I took the slick egg of butter and pressed it lightly in the center of Martha's forehead, just under the part in her hair.

We had talked many times about the fire and my husband and Miss Alice and her father and the creek and my loneliness and the town that was named for her. Now I just hummed against her hand. The butter fell into her lap. Martha sat, big and still, beside me, then lifted her hand from my mouth and took off her dress.

Her body spilled into the air around it. I whispered, "Worth everything."

Martha nodded. She knew this. She let her dress drop in a heap to the slatted floor and looked at me, then she pulled her palms along the folds of my sides.

I turned between her hands and opened the covers for her. She came under. We kissed. I smeared butter over her. I pushed it under her belly and licked it from her breasts.

She let one lump almost melt between her fingers before she slid it, slow grease, between my legs. We moved together for hours—swollen, glistening, languid and willing—sunk deep in butter and love.

We washed in the morning in the cold, shallow water of the stream.

Acknowledgments

I thank Sally Bellerose, Tryna Hope, Nina Crow Newington and Alice Sebold for critical early readings of the manuscript. The Valley Lesbian Writers Group—including Janet Aalfs, Toni Brown, Chaia Zblocki Heller, Susan Kan, Kathleen Kelley, Emma Morgan, Wendy Simpson, Gail Thomas— has been an ongoing source of community and clarity for me.

The Helene Wurlitzer Foundation and the Millay Colony gave me crucial time and space to write, and the Ludwig Vogelstein Foundation provided invaluable funding for my work on this book.

A generous community of friends—many of them lesbians from Western Massachusetts—has done so much to help me keep writing. The Lesbian Fat Activist Network and the Feminist Caucus of NAAFA (the National Association to Advance Fat Acceptance) have also offered me inspiration and support. The women of Spinsters Ink worked hard to bring this book into the world. I can hardly believe my luck in getting to work again with Gavin J. Grant and Kelly Link of Small Beer Press on this new edition. I thank my employer, the Center for Popular Economics collective, for flexibility and nerve. My family—Emmett Jordan; Mollie and Bill Stinson; Don, Barbara and Will, Marissa, and Emmett Stinson; Karen Stinson; Mike, Eva, Candace and Parker Stinson—are deeply important to me, and to my work.

I am grateful to live in such a varied world.

About the Author

Susan Stinson (susanstinson.net) is the author of four novels, including *Spider in a Tree* and *Martha Moody*, and a collection of poetry and lyric essays. Her work has appeared in *The Public Humanist*, *The Kenyon Review*, *The Seneca Review*, *Curve*, *Lambda Literary Review*, and *The Women's Review of Books*. She has taught at Amherst College, been awarded the Lambda Literary Foundation's Outstanding Mid-Career Novelist Prize, and has received a number of fellowships. An editor and writing coach, she was born in Texas, raised in Colorado, and now lives in Northampton, Massachusetts.

Also Available from Small Beer Press

"Like Jonathan Edwards, Stinson reads the natural world as well as Scripture, searching for meaning. But instead of the portents of an angry god, what she finds there is something numinous, complicated, and radiantly human."—Alison Bechdel, *Fun Home*

Spider in a Tree

a novel of the First Great Awakening by
Susan Stinson

"An honest imagining of everyday people caught up in extraordinary times, where ecstatic faith, town politics and human nature make contentious bedfellows."—*Historical Novel Review*

"An impressive chronicle conveying the intense spiritual yearnings that illuminate a colonial world of mud, disease, and fear." —*Booklist* (starred review)

9781618730695 · trade paper · 336pp · $17 | 9781618730701 · ebook

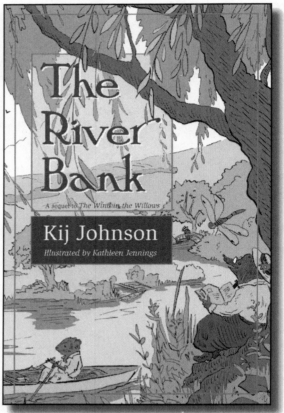

"Critics might say that *The River Bank* overly focuses on the two female characters, and that may be so. However, their presence brings a new flavor to *The Wind of the Willows* world, one that I was unaware was missing when I read it as a child. There are Victorian elements that are more pronounced with Beryl and Rabbit's presence, and yes, even feminist elements with the enterprising Rabbit solving problems in a most female way." — Lashawn M. Wanak, *Lightspeed*

9781618731302 · trade cloth · 208pp · $24 | 9781618731319 · ebook

"I'm re-reading after some years away, and loving the book even more than I did the first time! Marks creates a realistic society in which women are the dominant sex. I . . . love them and the world-building."
— Tamora Pierce, author of *Tempests and Slaughter*

"These books look at oppression, queer identity, and morality during a protracted civil war–definitely worth picking up."
— Gretchen Treu, A Room of One's Own

9781618730886 · trade paper · 329pp · $16 | 9781931520393 · ebook

Short story collections and novels from Small Beer Press
for independently minded readers:

Claire G. Coleman, *Terra Nullius: a novel*
NPR Best Books · Reading Women Award Shortlist

Karen Joy Fowler, *What I Didn't See and Other Stories*
World Fantasy Award winner

Greer Gilman, *Cry Murder! in a Small Voice*
Shirley Jackson Award winner

Elizabeth Hand, *Errantry: Stories*
"Elegant nightmares, sensuously told."—*Publishers Weekly*

Kij Johnson, *The River Bank: a sequel to The Wind in the Willow*
Washington Post Notable Books · *Seattle Times* Noteworthy Books · NPR Best Books

Karen Lord, *Redemption in Indigo*
Mythopoeic, Crawford, Carl Brandon Parallax, & Frank Collymore Award winner

Laurie J. Marks, *Air Logic*
"As the last note in a familiar melody, this book rings true." —*Kirkus Reviews*

Naomi Mitchison, *Travel Light*
"The enchantments of *Travel Light* contain more truth, more straight talking, a grittier,
harder-edged view of the world than any of the mundane descriptions of daily life you will
find in the science fiction stories."—*SF Site*

Abbey Mei Otis, *Alien Virus Love Disaster: Stories*
Philip K. Dick Award finalist · *Washington Post* Best Science Fiction and Fantasy of the Year

Sarah Pinsker, *Sooner or Later Everything Falls Into the Sea: Stories*
Philip K. Dick Award winner · *Milwaukee Journal Sentinel* Best Books

Geoff Ryman, *Was: a novel*
"A moving lament for lost childhoods." — *The New York Times*

Sofia Samatar, *A Stranger in Olondria*
"Samatar's sensual descriptions create a rich, strange landscape, allowing a lavish adventure to
unfold that is haunting and unforgettable."—*Library Journal* (starred review)

Our ebooks are available from our indie press ebooksite:

weightlessbooks.com
bookmoonbooks.com
smallbeerpress.com